A Player's Heart

By

Vivian Rose Lee

Preface

Sports doctor and physical therapist Dr. Zoey Howard did not want the spoiled, and egotistical Yazair Bryant, star running back for the Philadelphia Stallions as her patient. One thing she could not stand was egotistical football players. Because of his severe knee injury she was called in to get him back in shape and ready for the upcoming new season. On their first meeting she was not surprised he was hosting a party ten o'clock in the morning. It didn't matter to her, she was here to do her job and she was going to do it regardless of what Mr. Yazair Bryant thought.

However, Yazair Bryant knew the minute that the wisecracking and bossy doctor barged into his life that it would be forever changed. One thing he did not expect was her invading this player's heart.

Chapter One

Zola Howard known as Zoey to her friends stared aghast. Why didn't the housekeeper who answered the door tell her Yazair Bryant was entertaining? She glanced down at her watch. It was ten o'clock in the morning, and a party was in full swing beside the Olympic-sized pool. The party was complete with scantily clad women, some topless in the pool chased back and forth while men openly fondled what they offer. A few couples lounging in chairs in heated embraces like ornamental figures dotted around the pool while loud music played. There was empty overturned glassware, along with half-eaten food on tabletop's and trash thrown carelessly on the ground like confetti.

Zola shook her head. She realized right away that she made a mistake taking on this particular patient. Placing her bag and portable massage table near the doorway, she moved further out on the deck and down the stairs to poolside. The first thing she had to do is break up this little party. She scanned the area for Mr. Yazair Bryant. She rolled her eyes upward, shaking her head in disgust when she finally located him. There he sat in a wheelchair, a top-heavy silicone filled blonde sitting on his lap, nuzzling his neck.

Zola shook her head, at least, he had sense enough to keep his leg elevated. Her guarantee to the Stallion's owners is that she would get him back in shape, and that is what she meant to do. Taking a breath, she moved toward him stopping a few feet near his chair.

"Are you crazy get off his lap," Zoey shouted at the woman. The woman raised her head frowning.

"Who the hell are you?" She asked glaring at Zoey.

"Don't make me repeat myself," Zoey warned the woman her hands fisted on her hips.

"Yaz," the woman whined, "who is this bitch?"

Zoey didn't hesitate. She reached out grabbing the woman by her arm and snatched her off his lap. Yaz eyes squinted open.

The woman gasped. "How dare you touch me," the woman shrieked.

The music stopped. "Girl fight!" Zoey heard someone yell. All attention was on the little drama that was about to unfold.

"Who are you?" Yaz slurred.

Zoey ignored him for the moment. She glanced up and saw Nurse Sara and the housekeeper standing on the deck watching her.

"Now that I have everyone's attention, I'm here to inform you that the party is over. Get Out!" Zoey declared boldly.

A short round dark-skinned man came barreling through the crowd around Zoey.

"Who are you to come in here and break up a private party?" He screeched.

Zoey turned her eyes to appraised him from his head to his feet then gave him her most condescending look.

"Who are you?" She countered.

"I'm Calvin, Yaz cousin, and…,"

Zoey did not give him a chance to finish his thought.

"Well Cousin Calvin; do you live here?" She asked.

"No, but…,"

"You gotta go too," she interrupted turning her attention back to Yaz.

"You can't put me out. Who the hell are you?"

"That is none of your business," she said over her shoulder.

"Sara!" Zoey called, "bring my bag, please."

Sara grabbed her bag from where Zoey left it, ran down the steps, and quickly brought it to her remaining at her side.

"We ain't goin nowhere," Calvin said confidently.

"Oh you will be leaving and your freeloader friends too," Zoey replied with equal confidence.

She punched in some number and waited for a response.

"Hello David, I am here at Mr. Bryant's home, and they are partying like its 1999, I said they had to leave…," Zoey listened for a minute. "Okay." She handed the phone to Yaz. He listened and then handed the phone back.

"Get out!" He slurred.

"Yazy me too," the blond-haired woman whined.

"Especially you," Zoey grinned.

"You bitch," the woman cried and swung at Zoey.

Zoey ducked, swinging full fist connecting with the bimbo's chin. The woman stumbled back against Calvin.

"Now get out!"

With a lot of grumblings, his freeloading guest started moving. The housekeeper applauded as the procession of unwanted guest passed her to leave the house. Zoey followed with the wheelchair-bound man in tow, followed by Sara.

Yaz alcohol induced mind could hear her talking, but he could not comprehend what she was saying.

"How long has he been drinking like this?" Zoey asked Sara.

"None of your business," Yaz slurred.

"Oh be quiet drunkard!" Zoey spat as she pushed him through the open door of his first-floor bedroom.

Zoey stopped in the doorway of the largest bedroom she has ever seen.

"Whoa you could put my whole apartment in this room," Zoey said admiring the enormous room. It navy walls gave the room a warm feeling without being too dark. The rich wood floors shone like new money adding to the appeal of the room. Against the wall, a California sleigh bed that centered the room was enormous within it.

"Nice room Mr. Bryant," Zoey said continuing to the large bathroom that sat across the room.

"Where are you taking me?" He grumbled at her.

"Patience Mr. Bryant, I promise you will see in a second," she said sweetly.

Zoey was glad for the large fancy shower stall. She pushed the wheelchair into the shower and locked the wheels.

"What the hell...," Yaz slurred.

Zoey reached above him and turned on the faucets. The cold spray of water came from above and all sides.

"Yaz almost sprang from the chair cursing and sputtering. Zoey and Sara stood watching. Sara's hand covered her mouth shocked and stared at Zoey while she stood with her arms folded across her chest a smug smile on her face.

He was soaked through to his skin, "What the hell!" He shouted. "Both of you are fired, get out my house now!" He continued to yell.

Zoey tipped her head towards the door for Sara to leave; calmly she followed closing the door behind her. She could still hear him cursing and making a fuss.

Zoey looked at the concern on Sara's face.

"Don't worry, you will still have your job," Zoey assured her.

"You don't understand Zoey; he fired three others before me," Sara told her wringing her hands.

"Trust me; your job is safe."

"He fired you too," Sara reminded her.

Zoey shrugged. "He can't fire us, and you are now my nurse. He needs me; he just doesn't realize it yet." She smiled at Sara. "Is he alright; can he manage alone?" Zoey asked.

Sara nodded. "He bathes and dresses, I just change the dressing and try to give him medication that he won't take. I think that's why he drinks; to dull the pain in his body." Zoey nodded.

"It's awfully quiet, you think he's alright?" Sara asked.

Zoey started for the door just as it opened. With a towel draped around his waist, Yaz stood in the doorway with a crutch under his arm, sober and extremely angry if the expression on his face is any indication.

Zoey mouth fell open. She found herself face to face with a remarkably handsome man now that he was cleaned up and sober. Suddenly the room felt too warm. She felt her stomach cramp and her skin tingled. He had to be at least six-four. His warm chocolate complexion was flawless, his hair close-cropped in a neat cut, unusual gray eyes, narrow nose, full, sculptured lips, and chiseled jaw. His physique was incredible. His shoulders were broad with muscular pecs, tight abs, and torso perfectly toned leading down to a slim waist now wrapped with a thick white towel low on his hips. She didn't have to see the back of him she knew he would be just as impressive there as he was in the front. Zoey blinked rapidly trying to focus. What was wrong with her? She dealt with well-toned male bodies every day. So why did this moron's body affect her like none of the others?

Yaz hauled her roughly to him throwing his arm around her neck, interrupting her worthless musings. Without hesitation, Zoey wrapped her arm around his waist leaning her shoulder into his side to take the brunt his weight.

Zoey looked up at him. Yaz looked down at her.

"You're short," he said as she led him to the bed.

5

Zoey looked up at him with a slight smile. "You think."

Yaz looked down at her upturned face; beautiful, he thought. They made their way to the bed gingerly, and she gently helped him to sit. Zoey stood in front of him.

"Do you feel better?" Zoey asked.

"Hell no, my head hurts, my knee aches and I have pain in my butt," he said gruffly.

Zoey's elegantly shaped brow rose. Pain in the butt?" she repeated.

"Yes. You!" He stated.

Zoey mouth dropped open in mock surprise.

"Me," she repeated laughing and moved away from him.

"Sara can you give him some ibuprofen from my bag, please."

"I don't take pills," he protested.

Zoey smirked. "Yet you drink liquor to dull the pain in your knee, so you rather become an alcoholic or worse get alcohol poisoning than take a controlled medication for your pain and infection." Yaz shrugged.

Zoey turned away. "Like I thought a moron," she muttered under her breath.

Yaz frowned. "What did you say?"

"You need medicine," she answered innocently.

Yaz gray eyes narrowed. Who is the person who had the audacity to come barging in his house taking over him and his household? Now sober, he could better judge her with a clearer head. Yaz watched as she placed her bag on the floor; bending she pulled out some items handing them to Sara, who stood beside her. Yaz's eyes caressed the curves of her small body from her slender shoulders, the indentation of her tiny waist and nice, well-rounded hips and behind. Damn if she didn't look terrific in gray sweatpants and T-shirt.

Zoey rose and turned to him. She frowned. "Are you looking at my butt?" She asked brusquely.

"Yes," Yaz replied with a lopsided smile.

"Then stop it! Lie down please; I need to check...,"

"Lie down? Why and who the hell are you?"

"Didn't I introduce myself?" She snapped her fingers. "I always seem to forget that part. I'm Dr. Zola Howard, your sports doctor, and physical therapist," she supplied smiling.

"My what?" He replied confused. "Where's my doctor?"

"Sorry Mr. Bryant, but your doctor's been replaced. It seems the Philadelphia Stallion's owner thinks you are special so they called me in to take over and have you ready for training camp in six months."

"You're a doctor?" He asked in disbelief.

"Yes."

"And a Physical Therapist?"

"Yes, one of the best in the field," she replied boastfully.

"Says who?" Yaz challenged.

"My bank account," she said smiling proudly.

Yaz couldn't help but smile at her arrogant statement.

"So please lie back and put yourself in these small, capable hands and I'll take good care of you."

"Who have you treated Zola?" Yaz asked.

Zola stiffened. Nobody called her Zola. "Excuse me, Mr. Bryant, you may call me Miss Howard, Doctor Howard, I'll even accept Doc, but never called me Zola," she said glaring at him.

Yaz met the challenge. He owed her for putting him in the shower and sobering him.

"You're serious," he stated stunned by her sudden change in demeanor.

"Very. Now lie back, please."

"Yaz smiled and lay back quiet for now.

Zoey asked him various questions as she examined him. Yaz watched her closely. She was uncommonly pretty without a doubt, also stubborn, arrogant, spirited, sarcastic, gentle, and intelligent. A corner of his mouth lifted. Her head lifted, and their eyes met. Yaz kept his gaze locked on hers until his eyes lowered straying to her bow shaped lips. Her eyes never wavered, and then she gasped and moved away from him. Yaz felt as if a bolt of lightning passed through him. She felt it too; he knew she had. She was not as immune to him as she pretended. He smiled at her back. He admired the smooth oval planes of her face. The long dark hair that was pulled back in a ponytail enhancing her almond shaped eyes with the light brown irises outlined with a darker shade of brown that mesmerized him, along with high cheekbones, small nose, and full bow shaped lips. Her skin was the color of the hot dark caramel poured over ice cream. His stomach clenched in response. Correction, she was beautiful.

"Mr. Bryant tomorrow we will…,"

"What the hell is going on Yaz?" A man said barreling into the bedroom with the blond bimbo at his heel. She moved around the man and joined Yaz on the bed.

"Yazy," her tone whined, "are you alright?"

Zoey looked at the overweight, averaged height fair-skinned man, dressed in a suit too small that was in need of a serious ironing, and a briefcase in his pudgy hand. She then looked at the blond-haired woman that curled up next to Yaz on the bed jostling him. He flinched and the pain was visible on his face. Zoey's brows rose.

"Who the hell are you?" The man pointed in her face.

Zoey smacked his hand out of her face. "I am Dr. Howard, Mr. Bryant's doctor, and physical therapist. Who might you be?" She sneered.

"I'm his agent-slash-manager, and that's…"

"Let me guess Bambi," Zoey interrupted.

"Coco," the woman sneered.

"Rig--ht." Zoey turned her attention to the man in the room.

"Mr. Agent slash manager, Mr. Bryant is under my care; direct orders from the Stallion's owner, see him if you have any questions."

"I've already hired a physical therapist and…"

"And you get what 10%..." Zoey interrupted.

"Yaz means more to me than percentage…"

"Rig--ht," Zoey interrupted him again. "Well Mr. Agent slash manager I could care less how much Mr. Bryant means to you, for now, the parties stop; the drinking stops and the bimbo stops."

"Yazy did you hear what she called me," the woman whined.

Zoey turned to her. "Get off that bed before you jar his leg, can't you see he's in pain!" She shouted.

Yaz watched the scene unfold before him, and a smile curved his lips. His money was on the tiny Matilda the Hun. Coco slide off the bed stomped her Prada covered foot and glared at Zoey.

Zoey turned her eyes to Yaz, disgust evident in her glare. "Have you ever seen the movie

The Natural?" She asked him.

Yaz frowned. "You mean the movie with Robert Redford?"

"Yep, there's the blond, Memo Paris, from in the movie," she replied hitching her thumb towards Coco.

Yaz frowned not comprehending. After a minute, he laughed out. "I got it," he said chuckling. He looked at Coco and laughed harder. "Go home Coco," he said to her.

"Yaz I wanted to take care of you," she moaned with her overly painted lips pouted.

Zoey looked at her in incredulously. "Where are you from Trailer Park USA?"

"I most certainly am not, I attended college," Coco replied smugly.

"What did you major in, "How to get a Black athlete 101." Coco gasped. "Get out! When Mr. Bryant is up for the type of care you specialize in, I will personally call you," Zoey said tired of the drama.

"Look you!" The agent shouted.

Zoey turned to him. "That's Dr. Howard."

"Yaz has a photo shoot and interview that cannot be canceled.

Zoey turned to Yaz, who now was propped up with pillows his arms folded across his chest nonchalantly watching the scene about to unfold, a smile still on his face. Their eyes met.

"Cancel them, Mr. Bryant is in no condition to make any of those appointments," Zoey ordered.

"Who do you think you are?" The agents face reddening.

"I am Dr. Howard, Mr. Bryant's doctor, and physical therapist."

The agent looked at Yaz. "Help me here, Yazy."

Yaz shrugged. "My hands are tied Jimbo."

Zoey looked at the man smugly.

"Do I need to show you out or do you know the way, and take Bambi with you," she announced. Zoey stood beside the bed near Yaz, having a difficult time holding his laughter.

"Coco kneeled on the bed to kiss Yaz. Zoey cover his mouth with her hand just as she leaned over to kiss him.

"Sorry germs," she said with a smug smile that did not reach her eyes.

9

Zoey felt Yaz's lips curl up under her hand. Coco glared at Zoey and moved off the bed. Yaz pulled Zoey's hand away and entwined his fingers with hers. Zoey looked at their hands clasped together then up at him. Coco and the agent slash manager were fuming.

Yaz looked at Coco frowning. "What happened to your chin?" He asked Coco.

"She hit me," Coco whined. Zoey was beginning to think all Coco did was whine or maybe that was her natural voice.

Yaz looked over at Zoey astonished, then back to Coco. "When?"

"When she was throwing everyone out earlier," Coco stated.

Yaz eyes returned to Zoey.

Zoey shrugged. "She was sitting on your lap while you were in your drunken stupor. She could have caused more damage your knee," Zoey said defensively. "I pulled her off you; she then tried to slap me, I ducked, and she missed, so I checked her chin."

Yaz looked over at Coco and her bruised chin.

"I wanted to scratch her eyes out," Coco moaned.

Zoey raised a brow and folding her arms across her chest. "Please do," she invited.

"Jimbo let's go," Coco whined glaring at Zoey. "He will be better soon, and then you will be gone," she said pointing her overly ornate finger at Zoey.

"Give Bambi a gold star," Zoey said sarcastically. Sara sat on the chaise lounge discreetly laughing behind her hand as the agent and the bimbo left.

'Sara let's redress his knee, please, and we will be done for the day. Tomorrow we'll start your exerc'se regimen." She informed him.

Zoey had forgotten Yaz still held her hand; when she realized it, she snatched her hand away and glared at him. Yaz chuckled.

Chapter Two

Yaz lay on the massaging table as Zoey's magical hands worked his muscles to jelly. It still amazed him how this small woman had taken over him and his home. Miss Lilly, the housekeeper, loved her. All he heard was how incredible the doctor is. Even his temperamental chef sang her praises of grandeur. That wonderful doctor had the nerve to change his diet. He now was eating healthier meals, not the rich dinners he had hired Henri to prepare. On top of that, the doctor screened any visitors he had before they were permitted to see him. For the past few weeks, they acquired an undemanding professional camaraderie. However, it was still Mr. Bryant and Dr. Howard. He had asked her one day why she did not talk to him. She stated, "My mother told me if you didn't have anything pleasant to say just be quiet." He was not sure at first what that meant. Suddenly it clicked.

"You don't like me," He stated.

Zoey merely looked at him, cocked one eyebrow, and then lowered her head. The expression told him everything he needed to know and for some reason, it stung.

He recalled the day his cousin and a few of his partners came by to see him. Calvin was family, and that was the only reason she allowed him to visit.

He was in the middle of one of his sessions with the saintly doctor when Calvin along with his entourage barged into the workout room. He was sitting on the massage table, and Zoey was exercising his knee and massaging the calf of his injured leg. Calvin could not see Zoey sitting down on the stool in front of him.

"Hey Cuz," Calvin greeted loudly, "I came to see how you are dealing with dragon lady. I came by yesterday she said you had your quota of visitor and close the door in my face; you believe that?" The bitch got a lot of nerve; doesn't she know who I am?"

A chorus of baritone yeah has followed Calvin's words.

Yaz looked down at Zoey and she up at him.

Gently she removed his foot from her thigh and rose moving to stand beside him. A smirk was on Yaz's face when he looked back at his cousin, but the stunned look on Calvin's face was priceless.

"Yes, I do know who you are. You are the freeloader who comes by to receive his daily hand out and boasts I am the cousin of the best running back in the NFL. You suck up his popularity, and you drop his name to get attention as if you were out on the field running a football," she finished.

Calvin's mouth opened. His friends laughed.

Zoey glared at them. "And then you bring your freeloading friends along for the ride. Their mouths snapped shut.

Yaz lips curve slightly. All she said was true. Calvin was a freeloader along with his friends. They would come over and drink up his liquor, eat up his food, destroy his house always with a large group of people following him. He could see Calvin at the club telling people the after party was at Yaz's house. He never said anything to Calvin because of his aunt. They were the only family he now has with his mother gone. Sorry as Calvin is, he was still family. A pain knotted in his stomach. It always did when he thought of his mother. He thought about the sacrifices she made for him but did not live to see how successful he had become because of her premature death. Now Aunt Margaret, whom he puts up with, was reaping the benefits of his success that his mother should be enjoying, not his greedy, grabbing aunt and spoiled cousin. He remembered when he and Calvin were kids and how his Aunt Margaret used to tell his mother how he wouldn't amount too much because his mother spoiled him. Sure as a boy, he and Calvin got into minor trouble. Of course, Aunt Margaret blamed him because he was the oldest. When, in fact, it was Calvin and the boys he hung out with were the ones that were always in trouble. He only tried to stop Cal from doing some of the things they did. He was about thirteen years old, and the last time he got in trouble. His mother was called down to the police station to pick him up. When they got home, she tore him a new one and then lectured him about how hard she worked to provide him with a good life, and if he wanted a different life, he was free to go whenever he wanted. The chastisements hurt worse the spanking he received. That cured him. He excelled in school, was an exceptionally talented football player, and then got accepted to Penn State University on a full academic scholarship. He was an All-American football player, graduating with honor earning a BA in engineering. Since he loved football, he earned the first draft pick with the Atlanta Bueto's Franchise. Yaz looked at Calvin and then to the doctor.

Zoey went on to say. "By the way, freeloader, I guess you don't have a job?"

"You don't know what I got," Calvin bristled.

"That's what I thought," Zoey countered.

Calvin and his friends stood staring.

"Yaz you gonna let her talk to me like that?" He implored his cousin.

"Just go home Cal, come back tomorrow," Yaz said exasperatedly.

"You gonna take that bitch's side over family?" Calvin roared snidely.

"Don't call her that again Cal," Yaz warned as Zoey helped him from the table handing him his crutches.

Yaz leaned on her. "Remember what your Mom says," he whispered. She looked up at him with a genuine smile that enhanced her pretty face.

"Go home Cal, I'm tired," Yaz said and limped passed him. Zoey said nothing else as she opened the door so he could go through it. She held the door for his cousin and entourage.

"Y'all have a nice day ya hear," she said sarcastically smiling.

Yaz sighed contently as he lay on the bed. Zola Howard had spirit; he had to admit he strongly admired that. His mother would have liked her. Yaz sighed. For some reason today, his mother laid heavily on his mind. He looked at the digital alarm clock that displayed the time and date. March 15, his mother birthday. How could he forget this day? Since her death, he always took flowers to place them on her grave. The instant acute grief and sadness overwhelmed. Hot tears rolled down the sides of his face and he placed his arm over his eyes.

Zoey went to him with a pillow and placed it under his foot. Yaz growled. Zoey felt the tension suddenly in his body.

"Mr. Bryant are you alright, did I hurt you?" Her tone concerned.

"No," he replied gruffly sitting up on the side of the bed discreetly wiping his eyes. Zoey stepped back reaching out to help him. Yaz pushed her hands away impatiently and reached for his crutches. Zoey frowned confused.

"What's the matter?" She asked gently searching his face, her hand on his forearm. Her touch seemed to burn through his skin where she touched and Yaz shrugged her hand away. He didn't want her to be gentle and caring; it made him feel vulnerable.

"You are what's the matter is," he stated his tone acidity.

Zoey stepped back stung. Five minutes ago, he was defending her now he was biting her head off.

"I'm tired of you poking and rubbing on me, I'm tired of your bossiness, I'm tired of you sending my friends away, I'm tired of eating healthy food, and I'm tired of you!" He shouted at her.

Zoey heart leaped in her chest. She blinked the tears back that stung her eyes. Fury raced through her blood, her hands clenched at her sides. Zoey moved away from him to pack up her things.

13

"I hope you don't think this has been a walk in the park for me, you arrogant, overpaid moron. I thought I was helping you; your lifestyle was not helping your healing process, but hey, if you don't care then neither do I! I'm here to do a job! I didn't want to take on a spoiled overindulgent self-righteous jackass like you in the first place!" Zoey turned to pack up her equipment.

Yaz gray eyes were dark with fury.

"Get out of my house you overbearing, bossy pain in the ass, you're fired!" He shouted back.

"You can't fire me; you didn't hire me, but don't worry, I quit! You can kill yourself for all I care!" She yelled back.

Yaz watched as she put the reminding things in her bag. She walked to the open door. She turned and looked at him.

"Oh, and by the way, you don't have any friends!" She turned to walk out slamming the door behind her.

"I do have friends!" He yelled after her.

Zoey sat at her desk in her office going over her current cases. It had been two weeks since she and Mr. Bryant had their spat, still wondering why his words hurt her. She never cared what anyone thought of her, ever. Yet, his words cut her deep. In the weeks she treated him, his knee was beginning to heal, not completely, but it was better, and the pain had lessened. When he had his last x-ray, it showed a vast improvement in his injury. Never in her life had she given up on a patient, no matter how testy they got. He actually hurt her feelings. Maybe she was pushy and domineering; it was only because she cared. Her record of accomplishment proved that her former patients healed thoroughly and never had any more problems. The problem with Mr. Bryant was she was starting to like him. More than she should have.

They didn't say much to each other and when they did, it was not about personal things. Zoey smiled. He was smarter than she had originally thought. So why did he act like a spoiled moron for the public? There was more to Yazair Bryant than people knew. He had a compassionate side. She noticed the way he joked with Sara and Ms. Lilly always showing her the utmost respect. It was always yes ma'am or no ma'am, and he allowed her change

14

his diet and was genuinely surprised how delicious the food still was, but then Chef Henri could make anything taste terrific. He even once complimented her declaring she would make millions if she bottled her hands he joked promising to fund the project, and then he defended her when his cousin barged in calling her names.

So what happened she wondered? Zoey did not want to admit it, but she missed him.

Zoey looked down at the open files to try desperately to forget Yazair Bryant.

A knock on her door lifted her head.

"Zoey," her assistant called opening the door. "David Singleton and Dr. Olivetti are here to see you."

David Singleton, an ex-pro football player and owner of the Philly Stallions was a distinguished looking man, an aggressive entrepreneur, and her eldest brother Ellington's best friend, so she has known David all her life. Dr. Olivetti, an older man, the team doctor, and her mentor. The reason she decided sports medicine was her chosen career; when Ellington was an all-star pro ball player she was just a little girl, she remembered the year he got hurt. The injury ended his career leaving him with a severe limp. The decision to go into sports medicine was her only option. While raised with five older brothers, whom she loved more than life itself, and who play professional sports, she felt it was her duty to take care of the brothers.

When any of them got hurt while playing, she was there to nurse them back to health. Too bad, she was not old enough to help Ellington; if she were, he would not have that limp. The only consolation was when she finished her studies and earned her medical degree; she corrected what she could fix so he didn't suffer from too much pain from an old injury, and his limp was less severe. Later she returned to school and studied physical therapy. Now she was one of the best sports doctors in the city.

"Send them in," she instructed rising to stand in front of the desk. She didn't have to wonder what this visit was about; she bluntly told both men she would not deal with any more of their highly-strung spoiled asshole players. She went on to add, they didn't need doctors they needed nannies. When she resigned both men were not only upset, they were pissed. However, after talking to Yaz, he told them that he didn't want her back not that she would go back. When Ollie and David saw how much Yaz improved in the few weeks of her ministrations, they were impressed. She didn't care how impressed they were, she was

15

not going back.

"Gentlemen, please have a seat," she invited when they walked into her office.

David was not a man that hemmed and hawed, he got to the point and quickly.

Zoey leaned against the desk with his arms folded across her chest as both men sat.

Zoey I need you," David alleged.

"Hello David, Dr. Ollie," she greeted.

 "Give me a break Zo," David groaned.

"If this is about Mr. Bryant, forgets it David, I'm not interested. Didn't his manager hire him a reputable doctor and physical therapist?" She asked.

"If you call a therapist from Ling's massage parlor on Chestnut Street reputable, then I guess he did," Dr. Ollie stated disgustedly. "And don't get me started on the sleazy doctor he got to tend him; the man looks as if he should have lost his AMA card years ago."

"Reputable my ass," David scoffed. "The doctor is partying harder than the guest. However, that is not why I'm here. You need to know a little history about Yaz. He's not that person everyone sees. He really is a good man."

"What does that have to do with me, David?" Zoey asked impatiently.

"He needs you Zo," Dr. Ollie added.

"He has all he needs, his agent slash manager, his entourage, his freeloading cousin, his woman from Trailer Park USA, and his ego, so please don't play with my intelligence gentlemen."

"You're a stubborn woman Zoey Howard," David said exhaling.

A smile lifted the corner of her mouth. "Thanks."

"Okay Zoey, I need you," David finally said, "you are like my little sister, we're family."

Zoey rolled her eyes. "See David that's not fair," she groaned.

David smiled. "Just listen to me Little Bit, and then if you still refuse, I will leave it alone."

"Okay, okay," she agreed moving to take a seat behind her desk.

"Yaz wasn't as he is now. He was devastated after his mother died and it has changed the young man. I think he does the things he's been doing lately to hide the pain he feels. Let us face it; he has no one to talk to or confide in about how he feels. He needs someone who genuinely cares for him. His mother was a wonderful woman, and she and Yaz were very close. Her death hurt him deeply, and I don't think he gave himself time to mourn her loss. I think that he needs someone who genuinely cares about him if only just to listen to him."

Zoey was starting to feel sorry for Yaz now. "Damn it, David, I don't want to like him," she pouted. She could not help noticing that when they are together, he was a different person than the image he wanted people to believe. Zoey sucked her teeth. She didn't want to feel sorry for him, yet she did.

"So what do you need?" She asked knowing she couldn't turn her back on Mr. Bryant now.

"He's re-injured that knee, how, I don't know, but he has," Ollie said. "The last x-rays reveal more swelling.

Zoey was stunned. "But it was healing."

"I know," Ollie commented shaking his head.

"What about his physical therapist?"

"All I know is he no longer on his crutches and has been painting the town, if you will, limping. He's in pain, and he has been drinking heavily again according to his recently terminated nurse. The parties are endless." David informed her.

"He sounds hopeless and destructive to me. Ollie, what can I do?" She inquired.

"Whatever it is you did the last time he was under your care. Those people care nothing for him."

Zoey sighed. She already knew that. "You two like him that much?"

"Yes, plus he's worth 50 million dollars," David said.

Zoey sat silent for a minute. "Okay, but the second he starts giving me a difficult time I'm gone, got it," she said looking at both men.

They both grinned. David rose and hugged her.

"I owe you, Little Bit."

"That's right; you will. Can I get some backup this time, please? Because, when I start throwing people out it will not be done nicely. I'll go tonight."

"What do you need?" David asked smiling.

"The whole defensive starting line," she said earnestly.

"Done."

Later that evening Zoey and five of the Stallion's starting defensive linebackers went with her to Yaz's house that was packed with cars blocking the driveway and lined the street for at least a block. This must be some party she thought. When they entered the house was full to capacity. Women were running through the house, chased by men, others necking heavily in various corners of the room. Still she didn't see Yaz in all the chaos. She did see his freeloading cousin with two women on each one of his thick thighs. The room stank of stale liquor, cigarette smoke, along with the undeniable smell of marijuana hanging heavily in the air. Food and drinks overturned on the tables and the floor, and people threaded through it as if it were part of the flooring.

Zoey shook her head in disgust. She saw his agent with a large cigar between his teeth as he talked looking like a fake Don King. His back was to her when she approached him, so he had no idea she was standing right behind him. Zoey stood quietly, the five linebackers behind her. The freeloader also had not noticed her presence all that were in attendance of the soiree remained engrossed in his or her own debauchery.

Zoey heard the manager talking and boasting to another man, probably another sleazy partner.

"Yaz got to sign this contract and soon, if it gets out he has no official agent or manager, my ass will be cooked. David Singleton needs to mind his own damned business. Somehow the son of a bitch found out I don't have an official contract with Yaz and if word gets out, I stand to lose a great deal of money." The man paused taking a wheezing breath. "Although I know the boy would never let me go cause he knows if it weren't for me he wouldn't be living the life I got for him. What the hell has happened to the world when an honorable handshake between men holds no weight? It saddens me that loyalty and trusted have no place in business no more. Nowadays it's all about that all mighty dollars." The man said as he chewed on the cigar dangling from his mouth.

Zoey reached out to tap him on his shoulder when he continued his complaints. She halted and dropped her hand and listened closely. "If he finds out we have never had a contract he might be snatched up by one of those big time agents and I can't let my cash cow sign with someone else, he's worth too much money for me to let it be taken away. Brother got bills," he continued. "Did you know that almighty Duke Howard wanted to sign him two years ago? Yazy turned him down because of his devotion to me.

Zoey stiffened when she heard her brother's name mentioned.

"Why not tell him David Singleton is trying to push you out? Just tell him that he needs to renew the contract with you," the other man asked.

"The way it is now, Yaz trusts me to handle his finances, if it gets all legal, I'll be taking a big loss. I know Yaz. He will want to do it by the book. If I get him to sign the contract I got drawn up he will want to take it to some lawyer; I can't have that. So while, he is drunk, I can convince him to sign without batting an eye," The agent slash manager chuckled. "Can't have Yaz looking at the books now, can I?"

So that's it. This charlatan is using his intoxication to rip Yaz off. Zoey tapped him heavily on his back. He turned to see who was poking him in his back.

"What are you doing here? Yaz fired you!" He spat at her, his beady eyes narrowed.

"First of all, I quit, now I'm back. Where is Mr. Bryant?"

"As if I'd tell you," he chuckled mirthlessly.

"Fella's please," Zoey said with a smile glancing at the men behind her.

Two of the linebackers stood at his sides, grabbing him by each arm lifting the man off his feet. Fear etched on his sleazy face, and the man turned two shades of red.

"Where's Mr. Bryant?" She repeated the question.

"He's upstairs; busy."

"Throw him out," she said with a flick of her hand as she walked away.

Zoey waded her way through the debris and fornicators to the DJ's table and asked if she could make an announcement. The DJ gave her the microphone.

"Testing, testing, 1, 2, 3 ... May I have your attention," she spoke into the mike. However, no one responded.

"Turn off the music please, Mr. DJ," she asked politely.

The music stopped, and she heard a few hey's and vulgar words.

"Okay, now may I have your attention?" The linebackers moved behind her.

"The party is over, everybody, Get Out!"

No one moved.

Zoey looked at the freeloaders. "Please don't make me let these huge gentlemen help you out, I promise you, it will not be pretty."

"Who the hell are you?" Someone yelled from the crowd. One of the Linebackers stepped in front of the bold culprit, looking down at the cowering man. The invitees then started moving.

Calvin pushed his way through the departing guest. "Where is everyone going, the party is just getting started…?" He stopped talking when he saw Zoey, and she tilted her head and smile at Calvin.

"Hello Cousin Freeloader, it's time to go," she said sweetly. Zoey turned to the DJ. "Pack it up Mr. DJ," she said handing him the mike.

"Where's my money?" The DJ asked.

"Talk to Cousin Freeloader," she said leaving him.

Zoey walked up the staircase with her medical bag in hand.

Chapter Three

Yaz was lying on the bed and his knee throbbing like a headache. Coco was all over him trying to get a rise out of him. She wanted to take him in her mouth, which she did all the time, but he was not in the mood for that. Actually, he never had full intercourse with Coco and she always wondered why he never did. If she knew his reason, it would hurt her feelings for there wasn't a condom strong enough for him to have sex with Coco, and lately, he has been putting her off from oral sex. All he could think about was Zola Howard. He should have stopped her from leaving, but he was too prideful to ask her to return and was ashamed to admit that he missed her bossy, sarcastic way. After he had time to think about it, he felt ashamed of the way he attacked her. She did nothing to cause him to snap at her and she did not deserve what he said to her. Yet, still he refused to call her and make amends. Pride is a hell of a thing. The things she said to him still rang in his ears. Damn it, he missed her. After she had left, everything reverted back to where it had left off before she came into his life. Calvin, Jimbo, and the parties started up with a bang and the so-called endorsement deals that Jimbo schedule were a waste of his time only proving how unconcerned Jimbo was about his health.

Yaz knew his knee wasn't getting any better because the pain was more severe than before. When he told Jumbo he was not in the mood for these meetings, Jimbo convinced him the endorsements were too valuable to set aside, so he booked them one right after the other. Jimbo even convinced him that if he didn't want to lose his popularity he had to make the schedule public appearances. So again, he went along with Jimbo.

The doctor and physical therapist Jimbo hired were a joke. The therapist is no better than a glorified massage parlor masseur, and the doctor Jim found was eating him out of a house and home, and drinking his liquor like it was his own personal stash. Now Calvin was throwing parties seeming every night like he paid for them with Jimbo blessing. Miss Lilly, his housekeeper, and Chef Henri quit. She informed him that she was tired of cleaning the house after these parties, and Henri was not going to waste his gift on his uncouth visitor. His life was now a frigging mess.

Yaz winced. The pain in his knee was excruciating, and Coco was getting on his nerves.

"Coco, get off me, do you care that my knee is throbbing," he snapped.

"Of course, I care Yazy, I'm going to make you feel all better," she purred unbuckling his pants. He pushed her hand away.

"Well how about getting me some ice."

"I don't want you cool baby, I want you hot," she pouted before nuzzling his neck.

Yaz frowned. "Get off me!" He shouted pushing her away. "I'm in pain; I need ice for my knee."

"Let me get you a drink," Coco offered.

"I don't want a damn drink, I want some ice, is that too much to ask," Yaz yelled.

"Okay, okay," Coco said rising.

When she closed the door behind her, Yaz threw his arm over eyes, bearing the pain that trailed up his thigh.

Zoey eased open the door not sure what she would find. Yaz was fully clothed, his arm thrown across his eyes. Quietly she walked to the side of the bed. Gently she touched his arm. He lifted his arm, surprise evident in his gray eyes.

"Doc?" He groaned.

"Sh…," she said, "I know." Zoey reached into her bag, and pulled out a pair of scissors, cutting the leg of his jeans up above his knee. She looked up at him and shook her head when she saw how severely his knee had swell. She reached into her bag again and pulled out an ice pack, squeezing it between her hands until it popped and then shaking it. After a minute, she gently laid it on his knee.

"You're in pain," she stated softly.

Yaz nodded. Words did not come, but he was damn glad to see her.

"I understand how you feel about drugs, but a little something won't hurt, have you been drinking?" She asked gently.

"Not tonight," he stated.

"Do you want something for the pain?" She asked.

"Please."

Zoey smiled into his eyes.

"I'm glad to see you," he finally admitted.

"Really?" Zoey replied stunned.

"Yes really," he smiled at her. Yaz saw the tenderness in her eyes and then it was quickly gone. He watched as she prepared to give him a shot.

Right away she noticed the fatigue in his eyes. "You have not been resting," she accused.

"No, I haven't had a good night's sleep since you left," Yaz admitted.

"Well, tonight…,"

At that moment, the door flew open. Coco followed by Yaz teammates came into the room. One of the men held her clasped in his strong, capable hand.

"Yazy they were trying to throw me out," Coco replied pulling from the man and climbing onto the bed unmindful of his knee. Zoey saw him wince from the jarring and his eyes closed against the pain that Coco caused by jumping on the bed.

"Get off that bed, are you an insensitive ass as well as a moron. Can't you see he's in pain?" Zoey shouted angrily. Coco sneered but got off the bed.

Zoey looked at Yaz sheepishly. "Oh, I forgot. I broke up your little party."

"It wasn't my party," he admitted.

"Then why…" Zoey stopped. She was not going to comment.

"Hey fellas," Yaz greeted his teammates.

"Come on Yaz, it's time to get it together," one of his teammates said.

"You're right," Yaz agreed.

"Hello Bambi, it's always a pleasure," Zoey said sarcastically, "but you have to go."

"It's Coco," she replied through tight lips.

Zoey shrugged. "Same thing."

22

"Now I'm going to have to ask you all to leave, Mr. Bryant needs his rest," She said before addressing the five linebackers. "Thanks, fellas, I appreciate your help," Zoey said smiling.

"No problem," they chorused.

"Okay let's go, Bambi," one of the guys said.

"I'm staying, and my name is Coco," she shouted stomping her foot.

"Same thing," the others said.

"Yazy," she pouted.

"Go home Coco," Yaz said before he placed his arm over his eyes.

"It's either her or me Yazy," Coco threatened.

Yaz lifted his arm and looked at her.

"Bye Coco," he said covering his eyes again dismissing Coco.

"Your loss," she said and pushed past the linebackers.

"See you Yaz, get better because we need you," one of the linebackers said, "See you Zoey," they all said filing out of the room.

"Thanks again," Zoey said closing the door behind them.

This woman is something else, Yaz thought as he watched her from beneath the arm covering his eyes. Now alone, she quietly moved to the side of the bed.

"Are you ready for the shot?" She asked softly.

With his arm still over his eyes, he replied. "Yeah, go ahead."

Zoey lifted his arm from his face. After wiping his arm with an alcohol swab, she quickly gave him the shot then removed the ice pack from his knee to see if some of the swelling in his knee had gone down.

Zoey sat gently on the bed beside him and Yaz looked at her.

"Don't talk, just listen, the medicine will take effect in about five, or ten minutes so I will talk fast. David came to see me. He said you needed me, which is why I'm here and I will no longer interfere in your life. If you want to party fine, all I ask is that you wait until you are 100%, please. I will resume your therapy until you are cleared and then I will be out of our life." She started to rise.

Yaz reached out and grabbed her hand before she could pull away. Their eyes met.

"I'm sorry for what I said …,"

23

"No," she interrupted. "It's true; my brothers always say I'm too bossy."

Yaz smiled. "Brothers?"

"Yes, five older brothers," smiling fondly.

"I'm the only girl and the baby."

Zoey eased her hand from his.

"Tell me about them?" He asked closing his eyes. Zoey smiled and settled down beside him on the side of the bed.

"Well there is Ellington we call Duke, he is the oldest, Louis is known as Satch, Gillespie is known as Dizzy, Cabel we call Cab, and Ferdinand, whom we call Jelly; then it's me Zola, but everyone calls me Zoey," Zoey shrugged her shoulders sheepishly. "Mom and Dad loved jazz. What can I say?" She reached over him grabbing a pillow to put beneath his knee, only just now realizing he was still fully clothed.

"I'm sorry did you want to undress for bed?"

"I'm fine," he said.

"You sure, I'll help, you will be more comfortable."

Yaz nodded. "Thanks."

Zoey sat on the side of the bed and begin unbuttoning his shirt.

Zoey heart flipped, and her pulse leap like it always did whenever she saw his magnificent bare chest. One thing she can say about Yazair Bryant, he had the perfect, athletic body.

Yaz watched her slender fingers undo his shirt. He could feel the heat of her knuckles as they lightly brushed his chest. He sat up shrugging it off his shoulders. Her hand went to the waistband of his jeans. Yaz stopped her by taking her small hands in his. Zoey raised her head and looked at him questioningly. Their eyes locked.

He pulled her towards him. Yaz thought for sure she would pull back. He placed her hands on his chest and let them go. She stayed close. His hand reached to caress her cheek, her eyes closed, and then snapped open.

"Thanks for coming back," Yaz said softly. Before she could respond, Yaz hand closed around the back of her neck pulling her face close to his. His lips touched her lightly testing her reaction.

Just as he thought, warm and sweet.

He heard a faint purr escape her throat. His tongue traced her close mouth; she gasped parting her lips, and her tongue touched his. Yaz didn't hesitate to deepen the kiss slipping his tongue passed her lips and into her mouth. He gripped the ponytail in her hair pulling her close until they were chest-to-chest and he further deepened the kiss and to his surprise she responded and he felt the tension eased from her body. Was it her beautiful mouth or the effect of the medicine she had given him? No, his brain screamed, not yet let me taste some more of her. Vaguely he felt her hands cup his face deepening the kiss. The hand that gripped her head slowly slipped down, and then everything went black.

Zoey lifted her head and gazed at the now asleep Yaz. Her eyes slowly shut and she folded her lips into her mouth savoring his taste. She sat a while watching him. Gently she traced her finger over his lips. Shaking herself from her trance, she removed his pants. When Zoey had him down to his boxer briefs, her eyes trailed over his sculptured body. Her eyes lowered, and she stared mesmerized, even relaxed he was impressive. Zoey shook herself. Was she crazy ogling a client? Pulling the sheet to his waist, she covered him and then turned off the bedside light.

Zoey arrived early at Yaz's house. She took it upon herself to call Miss Lilly letting her know that she was back.

Ms. Lilly opened the door pulling her into her arms and into a fierce hug. "Oh baby girl I'm glad you are back I told you, he needed you," she replied.

Zoey gently untangled herself. "Miss Lilly, Mr. Bryant no more needs me than he needs a hole in the head. I'm just here to get him back on the playing field."

Ms. Lilly scoffed. "I know what I'm talking about Missy."

Zoey chuckled shaking her head. "Is he up?"

"Yes, and he's whistling," she said grinning.

"Whistling?" Zoey repeated confused.

A minute later Henri joined them. He took both her hands in his kissing them. "Mademoiselle we are so glad you returned Monsieur Yaz needs you."

Zoey shook her head. "No, he needs to get better, this is only temporary, you do know that," she said looking from one to the other.

Ms. Lilly and Henri exchanged a look but nodded that they understood. Zoey eyes narrowed as she looked at Ms. Lilly and then back to Henri.

"If you say so," Ms. Lilly replied easing the tension that was building.

"I'm not going to interfere with is diet anymore."

"He's not eating anyway," Ms. Lilly said shaking her salt and pepper head, "he hasn't since you left." Henri stood beside her nodding.

Zoey looked at each of them and shook her head. These two were hopeless.

"I will tell you what I think he should have," she conceded. After instructing them on his meal, Zoey went upstairs to greet her patient.

In the shower/steam bath, Yaz sat on the bench his body more relaxed than he could remember. He felt a lightness he had not felt in a long time. He closed his eyes laying his head back against the wall behind him. His mind was full of thoughts of Zoey. He could still taste the sweetness of her lips, and it still surprised him that she responded, or maybe he imagined it with the shot she had given. No, he decided she was very responsive and a satisfied smile curled his lips.

Zoey entered the room. She did not hear the shower. Perhaps he was finished bathing. She went about setting up the massage table when she glanced at the bed and a sensation she never felt before flooded her with a feeling she could not describe. The feeling was so acute that it reached into the depths of her belly astounding her inwardly and she prayed he was too groggy to remember the best kiss she has ever experienced. When she got home, she vigorously chided herself. That kiss should have never happened. He is her patient for goodness sake, and she never fraternized with her patients; it was her number one rule. So what was it about Yazair Bryant that made her break her most cardinal rule? He was not so special, hell, she didn't even like him, did she? Zoey groaned and dropped her head.

Yaz stood leaning against the doorway watching her, his eyes taking in her petite body. He loved the way her jeans hugged her well-rounded hips and the smallness of her waist. Instantly he could imagine her riding him as his hands held her waist guiding her up and down his manhood, and with the thought of Zoey riding him caused a quickening in his loins. It would not be a good idea to let her see his towel tented. Yaz quietly stepped back into the bathroom and splashed cold water on his face. Gazing into the mirror at himself, he wanted Zola Howard as he has never wanted anything in his life. Drying his face, and satisfied his libido was cool, he went to the bedroom. Zoey was spreading a sheet on the massaging table, oblivious to his presence.

"Good morning," his husky baritone voice greeted quietly behind her.

Zoey turned sharply. Her breath caught in her chest. He was as beautiful as she remembered, she thought as her eyes leisurely trailed his towel-clad body. Not that, she was unaware of his body in the past, it just seem after the kiss she was more acutely aware of his virility. Zoey closed her eyes slowly. Get it together girl, she chided herself. She has seen him wrapped in a towel plenty of times on her previous visits, she knew he had broad muscular shoulders and chest, washboard abs, and hard, muscular well-shaped legs. So what's the problem? Get it together jacktail, she chided herself again. Her eyes opened. Good morning," she said hoping her voice didn't sound as tight as it felt.

Zoey turned her back pretending to be busy smoothing the sheet on the table.

"I think you should just rest today," she said trying to sound like the no nonsense doctor she is. "First a massage, and then just rest your knee today. You have been on it far too much. And where is your crutch?" She asked looking around the room. "You have to keep the weight off of it for a few days." Zoey knew she was babbling she just hoped she didn't sound like an idiot. He made her nervous, which was unusual because she was never nervous around him before last night. Her eyes closed tightly. "Get a grip Zo, get a grip," she scolded silently before turning with a smile on her face. She wished he say something instead of standing there staring at her.

Her eyes met his and her heart slammed against her chest. She was dumbstruck.

"You want a massage before breakfast?" She asked softer than intended.

Yaz gave her a knowing lopsided smile. "Yes, but whose cooking, Ms. Lilly and Henri quit?"

Zoey turned her eyes away before answering him. "I called them back, and breakfast is now being prepared as we speak," She affirmed.

Yaz smiled widened.

"You don't mind do you? I know I…" her voice faded as Yaz limped towards her.

"I'm glad you did. I'll see them later," he told her.

Zoey eyes widen as she watched him and she never felt so uncomfortable in her life. The way his voice caressed her made her feel all melted and warm. Yaz kept limping forward, his gray eyes dark, eyeing her with a sensual sparkle to them, as his muscles rippling with step he took. Zoey felt as if she were suffocating and took an unconscious step back only to be halted by the massage table behind her. Her fingers gripped hard on the table as her eyes took in his handsome face.

"Doc?" He said questioningly.

Zoey chuckled. "You ready?" She asked moving from the table.

Yaz nodded and lay face down on the table.

With slightly trembling hands, she covered his lower half with a folded sheet. When he was covered to her satisfaction, Yaz removed the towel tossing it to the floor. He quietly laid his head on folded arms and Zoey took a deep breath, squeezed the oil into her hands rubbing them together longer than necessary. Get a grip she repeated to her. You have massaged him several times, what's the big deal. She placed her hands on him and begun to rub his smooth, broad back applying just the right amount of pressure.

"Mm…," Yaz moaned huskily.

Zoey eyes followed her hands as she trailed down his back to this tapered waist. She felt a sudden heat invade her body making her all languid and breathless and her eyes slowly closed as she allowed her senses to take over. Her hands slowed as she stroked his velvety silk skin while she imagined his hands stroking her. She moaned softly while she gently moving her warm slippery hands in lazy circles lost in her fantasy.

Yaz immediately felt the difference in her touch, the weight of her finger were now lighter, slower, and erotic. He lifted his head turning to look at her. He watched as her tongue darted out lazily tracing her lips. Below his waist, his manhood jerked awakening. A smile curved his sensual lips.

Yaz rolled to his side pulling the sheet to cover him. Zoey's eyes widened meeting his sultry gaze and dropped her hand. He reached up with one hand gently taking her hand in his. He pushed himself up sitting pulling the sheet across his lap while he held on to her. Stunned Zoey watched as he maneuvered her to stand between his legs mesmerized by the blatant sensual look in his eyes. Slowly her eyes lowered to his mouth as his hands eased around the back of her head pulling the elastic hair band from her ponytail tossing it aside. Zoey felt his finger slipped through her thick hair pulling it to frame her face. His eyes gazed at her face. "Beautiful," he whispered. With no difficulty, he brought her forward to meet his mouth. When his lips touched, she gasped. Zoey felt a shock run through her entire body, now breathless and overwhelmed by him as if her muscles were pure jelly. This kiss was nothing like last night and she prayed it never ends. Suddenly there was a tingling and tightening sensation deep in her stomach and a thickness between her thighs. Her mouth open instinctively and he smoothly slipped is tongue inside, her senses savoring his taste. This was no rushed kiss. He was taking his leisure tasting her. Of their own accord, her hands slipped over broad shoulders pressing herself closer as his name tumbled around in her mind. A slight moan of pleasure escaped her throat, and he pulled her closer. She felt the warmth of his large hands as they pressed into her back. Temptation and desire coursed through her at a rate that had her lightheaded. His extreme hard body enveloped her in the incredible warmth and softness of him and she was entirely lost in this man's embrace.

Neither heard the door open so engrossed they were in the sensual kiss. Yaz was the first to pull away when he heard Ms. Lilly loudly clearing her throat, a smile on her face and a tray in her hands. Zoey hazy eyes were still on Yaz. She still didn't know Ms. Lilly had entered the room.

"Breakfast is served," Ms. Lilly said cheerily.

Zoey jumped startled, looking at Ms. Lilly with wide embarrassed eyes, the sensual fog quickly lifting. By the grin on Ms. Lilly face, Zoey knew she had caught them. Zoey turned away mortified that Ms. Lilly had caught her in the arms of a naked Yaz, well half-naked.

"Sorry children, if I had known…,"

"No. No, Ms. Lilly, it's not what you think," Zoey stammered feeling the need to explain.

Yaz looked at Ms. Lilly, who was now grinning. "Should I come back later?" She asked mischievously.

"No, Yes," Yaz and Zoey spoke at the same time.

"Just leave it on the table, Ms. Lilly," Yaz said with a chuckle.

Placing the tray on a small round table, Ms. Lilly grinned at them before turning to leave.

"Miss Lilly," Yaz called to her. "I'm sorry for everything, and I'm glad you and Henri are back, thank you," Yaz said sincerely.

"Humph, don't thank me, thank Zoey," she replied closing the door.

"I'd better go. You should eat, and get some rest. And whatever you do stay off that leg as much as possible. Tomorrow…,"

Yaz caught her hand pulling her to him. Zoey stiffened. "Have breakfast with me? He interrupted.

"I'm sorry, I did not finish your massage."

"Yes you did, I'm very relaxed now," he smiled. "Come on, what are you afraid of?" He challenged.

"Please, afraid of what; you?" She countered trying to pull her hands from his.

Yaz chuckled tightening his grip on her hand.

"Okay, now can I have my hand back?" Yaz released her hand. Zoey pulled away to get his crutches and robe handing it to him and turning her back to give him privacy until he was covered. Zoey handed him the crutches. He moved off the table with her help. To distract herself, she pulled a chair from the table and helped him sit and prop his foot on another chair. Zoey lifted the covers from the tray and it looked as if Ms. Lilly made enough food for five people. Zoey shook her head and served them the turkey ham steak, scrambled eggs, grits, toast, and decaf coffee before she sat across from him.

Silently Zoey sat across from him. She lowered her head and blessed the food.

"Hungry?" She asked.

"Mm... starved."

She watched him literally inhale his food. "When was the last time you have eaten?" She asked frowning. He shrugged his broad shoulders.

Zoey chuckled softly shaking her head taking a bite of her food. She was quiet, which was a first for her. Usually, she had so much to say all the time, however now she was somehow at a loss for words. She looked across from him, and her heart lurched in her chest when their eyes met. What the heck is wrong with her? She should be able to handle this for goodness sake she was twenty-five years old. The mistake she made was allowing him to kiss her again, in his bedroom while naked, well almost naked. After that kiss last night it was all she thought about until sleep finally claimed, then waking this morning with the same thoughts. If the medication had not kicked in when it did, it was no telling what predicament she would have found herself. If Ms. Lilly hadn't come in when she did, she would have found herself in trouble again. The bad thing about it all is it was the best thing she has ever felt for the first time.

"Are you alright?" Yaz asked. "You have this strange look on your face."

"I've never been kissed before...uh...that not what I meant to say...," Zoey groaned her hands covering her face. "I didn't mean to say that, I..," she paused sighing she gave up. Zoey peeked through her spread fingers to see Yaz grinning at her. She lowered her hands. "Kill me now Lord, just kill me now."

"Is that good or bad?" Yaz asked chuckling.

Zoey frowned. "We should have never done that, that's all," she snapped stuffing a piece of toast in her mouth.

"Why?" Yaz asked his beautiful eyes shining with contained laughter.

Zoey rose swiftly from the table slammed her napkin on her half-full plate. "You're my patient daggumit!" She snapped.

"Daggumit? What does that mean? Never mind I don't want to know," Yaz chuckled.

Yaz laughed as he watched Zoey pace the room incoherently mumbling.

"Are you seeing anyone?" He asked breaking into her rambling, hoping he didn't regret the question.

She stopped and glared at him. "What has that to do with...?"

"Dating?"

Zoey glared at him. "I hope you can manage because I'm leaving, get some rest today; we are going to work especially hard tomorrow," she replied going to the door. "I'll tell Ms. Lilly she can get the trays.

"Chicken," Yaz shouted through the door and laughed. "See you tomorrow!"

She was like a scared little rabbit when it came to her personal life. She is so skittish, and it would not surprise him if she were still a virgin. Chuckling and shaking his head Yaz hobbled to his bed.

Still highly annoyed for her weakness, Zoey stomped into her rooms. Actually, she was on the first floor In-law or au pair suite with a sunroom, a living room, bedroom and large bath with a private entrance. Ellington insisted she reside with him after she graduated from college when she had wanted to have her own apartment in the city, but being the baby of the family and the only female she was outvoted by her five older brothers because they were afraid for her safety. So she had to move to Cherry Hill in New Jersey.

"Daggumit," she cursed. When she realized she rushed out of his house so quickly, she left all her equipment. Thankfully, she was free of any appointments today having cleared her calendar to accommodate the spoiled Yazair Bryant. What was it about that man that made her heart flutter and her stomach drop as if she were on a wild roller coaster?

Her phone vibrated at her side. "Yeah!" She nearly shouted into the phone.

"Hey Zo, are you alright?" Duke her brother asked concern in his tone.

Zoey took a deep breath. "Yes, I'm fine just a tough day," she answered.

"Okay, come on up Pud, I made lunch," he invited.

Zoey groaned. It must be the housekeeper's day off. Duke could not cook if the recipe were in his face, but rather than hurt his feelings she would go up and eat. Duke was thirty-five years old, for god sakes, it was time for him to settle down and find himself a wife that could cook.

Zoey sat at the kitchen counter with Duke. Thankful lunch was turkey sandwiches and canned soup.

"What got you so moody Pud," Duke asked in between bites of her sandwich.

Zoey shrugged her shoulders. "I've been getting Yazair Bryant ready for camp," she replied.

"That's right he messed up his knee badly, didn't he?"

"It was pretty severe, but before I could help him heal I had to clean house. After his injury, the parties started when I started I put a stop to them. I don't think Mr. Bryant's friends care for me. He even fired me, after that the partying resumed. I was determined I wouldn't go back, but David practically begged me so I did it for him, and again I had to clean house."

"Being bossy again huh Pud," Duke said chuckling.

Zoey mouth dropped open. "No, Yazair Bryant is an arrogant, out of touch jock, who cares about nothing!" Zoey shouted. He can't even see when he is being used by his so called manager and cousin.

"Who's his manager?" Duke asked curiously.

"I call him agent slash manager; I think Mr. Bryant calls him Jim or something. When I broke up the last party, I overheard the agent slash manager talking. He doesn't even have a contract with Mr. Bryant and since David is putting pressure on what's his name, he's trying to get Mr. Bryant to sign some papers he had drawn up. I think that sleazy man has been cheating Yaz…; I mean Mr. Bryant."

"Really, did you tell Yaz?" Duke asked concerned. He hated to see athletes hooked up with these ostensible sleazy agents. He remembered when Yaz was in college and he was interested in the talented player, but he was told he already had representation.

"No it's none of my business," Zoey replied defiantly.

"Come on Pud, if the man's being cheated and you know it, it is your business," Duke reprimanded.

Zoey frowned at her brother. She knew how passionately Duke felt about athletes being taken advantage of. "Oh alright I'll tell me tomorrow," she huffed rising from the bar. "Just so you know, Mr. Bryant and I don't always see eye to eye and if he tells me to mind my own business, it will be your fault." Rolling her eyes and she left the kitchen.

Chapter Four

Zoey arrived the next morning to Yaz sitting down to a large, hearty breakfast.

"Hungry?" She asked when she entered the room.

"Mm… starved," he replied looking over at her with a sensual light in his eyes. "Join me," he invited.

Zoey sat across from him, served herself and started eating. Her heart was pounding like some young girl.

Yaz grinned at her. "You never did answer my question?"

Zoey looked up at him frowning. "What question?"

"Are you seeing anyone?"

"No. Why?"

"Dating?"

"Not as much as I should be," she replied nonchalantly.

Yaz brows inquiringly as he took in her statement.

"I don't date much," she said shrugging. Actually, she didn't date at all.

Yaz was inwardly elated. He smiled.

Zoey stared at him. She had never known a man as attractive as Yaz, even more so when he smiled, but that's all he had. His inner self needed adjusting. David said he was a good person and maybe he was. Her only question was why did he try to be something he was

33

not?

Uncomfortable with his line of questions, Zoey turned the tables. "You have a girlfriend," she stated.

"Who?" Yaz frowned.

"Barbie," she spat.

Yaz chuckled. "Coco is not my girlfriend."

"Really? Then why is she always all over you?"

"You have me there, but I have no ties to Coco or any other woman." At least not the woman he thought he loved long ago. He hadn't thought about her in a long time.

"But Coco…,"

"Has her purpose," Yaz interrupted.

Zoey groaned. "I do not want to hear this," she said rising from the table.

"I never slept with Coco," he stated.

"It's none of my business," she stated and moved away to unpack her equipment.

For some reason, her dismissive attitude bothered him.

"I want you to know I was never intimate with her, my agent started bringing her around after I got injured, that's how she came about."

"Talk about sleazy," Zoey muttered.

Yaz frowned. "What's wrong with my agent?" Yaz asked defensively.

"If you can't see it, he must be alright with you," she stated noncommittally.

"Jim has been with me since high school," he stated.

Zoey didn't want to get into this with him. Duke was an agent, so she did have some knowledge of the field.

"I owe him," Yaz said after a minute.

Zoey stopped what she was doing and faced him, her hands planted on her hips.

"Then tell me Yaz, why is it that you are already on a new team after two years?"

"Well…,"

"I'll tell you. Because your agent is a sleazy cheat," she said through clenched teeth.

Yaz body stiffened, now angry. She didn't know Jim or the history they have together.

"You don't know Jim."

"Maybe, but I do know he cares about money, your money and you are so busy trying to be a big shot, ole Jim is ripping you off," she yelled at him.

Yaz turned his back to her. What the hell does she know about his manager?

"You're wrong!" He shouted. Jim cares about me!

"Really, well if he cared so much about you, why are you still in pain after I left you? And why did you do all those appearance and interviews knowing you should have been staying off that knee? I know you got a 50 million contract; how much did Jim get and what about your endorsement deals, how much did you earn from them?"

"What the hell are you talking about; I did not get a 50 million dollar?" Yaz looked at her confused. He did not want to hear any more from her.

Zoey continued. "Did you know you have no contract with this Jim?

"Of course, I have a contract," he countered.

Zoey chuckled mirthlessly. "I heard him telling one of his constituents at the last party, to keep you drunk, so you would sign a contract. And you trust him?"

"How do you know its 50 million?"

"David mentioned you were worth 50 million, maybe more, Duke confirmed it."

"Duke Howard, the biggest sports agent in the NFL?"

"Yep and my oldest brother," she replied proudly.

Now Yaz was angry. He came to his feet, not caring about the crutches.

"No!" Zoey shouted rushing to help him. She wrapped her arm around his waist. "Stay off that knee!"

Yaz looked over at her as they sat on the side of the bed now quiet.

Yaz was deep in thought wondering if what Zoey said is true. Was Jim cheating him? He didn't know anything about 50 million from the Stallions. Jim reported he got a 30 million dollar contract. He had known Jim all his life, there was no way Jim wouldn't cheat him. Yaz glanced over at Zoey.

"Do you think he's cheating me?" He asked.

"Yes I do," she replied simply looking directly into his eyes.

Yaz shook his head not wanting to believe this. "Why would he? I give him a decent percentage."

"Greed," Zoey said rising.

Yaz caught her hand and looked up at her. "How can I know for sure?"

"You never sat in on the negotiations?"

"No," he replied softly. "I trusted Jim."

"Talk to David and see what was negotiated. I'll have Duke find out about some of those so-called deals and endorsements."

"If sleazy Jim got you 50 million what do you think Duke would have gotten you without endorsement deals. And if Duke were your agent you would not be acting all high and mighty, because Duke would have humbled your butt quickly."

Yaz pulled her down to sit beside him again. "Duke wanted to rep me when I was in college, but I was loyal to Jim."

Zoey shrugged. "Well if you are, then stay with him. I think Jim owns you; you just don't know it."

"No one owns me," Yaz said adamantly.

Getting up again, she said. "Lay back let me check your knee."

While Zoey silently exercised his leg, Yaz was deep in thought. Maybe Jim did feel that way, he never asked him what he wanted. If Jim said to do something he would simply obey.

"How does that feel?" Zoey asked invading his thoughts.

Yaz looked at her thoughtfully. "Help me to get stronger Zoey."

Zoey smiled.

After his session with Zoey, he thought over her question. She made him think of the things he pushed back in the crevices of his psyche. The question Zoey should have asked was, had he ever been in love? The answer would have been a resounding yes, not that he would have told her. There had been a special woman in his life at one time.

His heart leaped and knew it was love at first sight. The petite, fair skinned woman with dainty flawless feature and long dark straight hair that brushed the small of her back that reminded him of the porcelain doll his mother kept in a glass dome on her dresser. She was beautiful. She was so fair she could have easily passed as a Caucasian. However, Trisha Devereaux would haughtily shut down all who said she was white and informed them that she was not white, but a beautiful Creole woman from a wealthy family with old money from New Orleans. They had a couple of classes together and that was when he got the opportunity to meet her when the professor sent her to him to be tutored in calculus. The tutor/student relationship they had quickly turned into exclusive dating. In love and happy, Yaz thanked God for Trish. He would never believe he could get someone as beautiful and perfect as Trisha Devereaux. As the relationship grew so did his love for her eventually taking it to the next level. He was far from being a virgin, but the first time they made love was mind blowing and soul stealing. His only regret was he had not been her first. She was his queen now and that was all that matter. It didn't matter that his teammates didn't care for her, they thought her bouche. Granted she was spoiled and had to have her way in all things, and felt he was the only man to give all her heart desires. He knew once he went pro he would be able to give her anything she wanted. When was the recipient of the Heisman Trophy, then drafted by the Atlanta Bueto's and maintained a 4.0 GPA graduating top of his class he knew he was on his way. He knew how proud his mother is of him and he was humbled. Jim, his trusted friend, controlled his career and had his back and Trish Devereaux loved him. She may not say the words, but he knew she did. For him, life was good and could only get better. At least, that was how he felt after graduation, the day that marked the beginning of his end. The day was beautiful; the arena was full to capacity with invited friends and family proudly celebrating their child's achievements. After the commencement service ended, and the cap and gowns were removed, every graduating student was ready to party. His mother and Jim were taking him to a special dinner and Trish's parents were hosting a small party at the Ritz Carlton where they were registered and he would meet up with Trish later. When he was introduced to Mr. and Mrs. Devereaux before the commencement, he couldn't help feeling the cool reception he received from her parents. Trish was the spitting image of her mother and Mrs. Devereaux was beautiful, her father a light skinned medium height man doted on his lovely wife and beautiful daughter.

After safely getting his mother home, Yaz felt happy and lighthearted knowing he would soon see the other important woman in his life. He never thought he could be so happy. He was worth 30 million, had the degree he worked hard to achieve, a starter for the Super Bowl Champion Atlanta Bueto's, and a beautiful woman who he wanted to make his wife. Four years with Trish was not enough, he wanted a lifetime of her love. Now if she became his wife his life would be perfect.

The party was under way in the suite when he arrived. Yaz waved and greeted his frat brother and teammates. With his height, he could easily see over the heads of the invited guests in search of his soon to be bride. He patted his pocket to ensure his surprise was still there. Finally, he found her on the terrace with her mother. Although her mother seemed chilly at their introduction, Yaz was sure and determined that he would win her heart. Mrs. Devereaux and Trish's backs were to him. Quietly with a light heart, he approached the open French doors. Yaz paused and stood in the open doorway admiring his future wife and her mother. He started to make his appearance known when her mother started to question her.

"What did you say his name is cherie'? Her mother asked.

"Yazair Bryant, he's very handsome is he not? Trish replied. Yaz started grinning behind them like an idiot.

"Yes, my love, very handsome, but he's so black."

Chuckling Trish said, "Oh Momma, he is not. He's, at the least, a medium brown."

Her mother sucked her teeth. "He's too dark for this family, baby." Her mother looked at her suddenly alarmed.

Trish smile faded. "What, Momma, what is it?'

"You're not thinking of marrying him, Chérie?

Chuckling, "Oh Momma no, Yaz is like a--pet, you know for protection. He's very rich now that he has been drafted to play pro football. He spoils me terribly, even when he had nothing, he made sure I got everything and anything I wanted. He's very sweet."

Oh, Chérie' you are beautiful," her mother said caressing her cheek, "who wouldn't want to give all to you. Do you love him?"

"Oh Momma, don't be silly. Of course, I don't love him, I know he's too dark to be in our elite circle and if we had children--I shudder to think," she said with a shiver. "Anyway, I'm not made to be a football player's wife, I'm First Lady stock," she boasted haughtily.

Her mother grinned. "Yes, you are darling, I have taught you well," she replied proudly. "You know Senator Benson's son just graduated Harvard, maybe you and he can get together sometime."

Yaz had never been so hurt or humiliated in his life. All she saw him as was her pet, her protector. Incredible, For four years he crawled at her feet, giving her things he could never afford. She never loved him. How could she not love him? The way they made love was incredible; no one could make love like that if they didn't have feelings. Stunned, he could move. His face felt numb and his mind was blank.

Trish and her mother turned to leave the terrace. The looks on their faces were comical. One look at Yaz told them both he heard every word they said.

"Yaz," Trish whispered.

"Thanks, Trish," he choked out. At that moment, he vowed never to love again. Without a backward glance, he walked out of the door.

Chapter Five

Yaz and Zoey worked tirelessly to get him 100% physically. It was hard work, but with dogged determination and his love of the game he was going to get his career and his life back. Through all of the drama and occasional arguments, an unspoken bond seemed to grow between them. Although they could laugh and sometimes talk, they would go weeks without any major disagreement, keeping everything strictly business. Yaz admired Zoey Howard's strict demeanor and giving up was not an option. Finally, he was given a clean bill of health, and Zoey brought in her best physical trainer to get his body prepared for the vigorous training camp. Now in their six months of rehabilitation, Yaz was more than ready to get back to playing football.

As Zoey had promised Duke did look into his finance, and it was found that Jim was not only getting 20%, but also the money paid to Yaz for his appearances and endorsements. His contract agreement with the Stallions was $50 million as Duke reported. The power of attorney Yaz gave Jim authorizing him to sign his name when needed. He pulled out his copy of his contract. The forged replica of his contract that Jim had drawn up and presented to him stating the agreement of $30 million a year with the option of renewal at the end of three years. Yaz remembered that day well. They had celebrated for two days when the Stallions decided to pick him after he was traded by the Buetos. Jim assured him he did not have to attend the meeting promising to take care of everything that was in his best interest as he always has because he trusted Jim. At first, Yaz felt hurt and betrayed by Jim's treachery. Yaz shook his head in utter disbelief as the truth came to light that he had been used by the man he looked up to as a father. Now all he could feel is the anger that threatened to choke him.

Duke suggested he have Jim charged with embezzlement, but he opted to face him and take back what he stole. The good thing now is that Jim still was unaware that he had knowledge of his deceit, and that gave him the upper hand. Since he never had a contract with Jim, Yaz signed with Duke without hesitation. Duke offered to take care of Jim and inform him of the changes in his career, but Yaz refused the offer. He needed to deal with this on his own. Some time later he discovered that Jim and Calvin were in cahoots. Their goal after he had gotten injured was to keep him drunk and unconscious. The same people who partied at his house were more than happy to tell him that Jim and Calvin bragged about how they used him. Saying they were going to get what they can before he lost it all. After the knowledge he now held against them, Yaz refused to take any calls from Jim or Calvin and refusing them entrance to his house. Ms. Lilly along with her Louisville Slugger was more than happy to tell them. As was the norm, Calvin went whining to his mother as he always did when they were boys if he had something Calvin wanted. Yaz grimaced as he recalled Aunt Margaret yelling at him on the phone.

"I want to know why you will not see Calvin?" she screeched so loud Yaz had to pull the phone from his ear. There was no "hello nephew how are you?"

"I'm busy Aunt Margaret," he replied through clenched teeth. He had to remember she was still his elder and his mother sister.

"Don't you get smart, boy, you ain't never too busy for family. Calvin is like your brother; we are blood and I will not allow you to turn your back on us. Don't forget I took you and your mother in when you had nothing but the clothes on your back. If your simple ass mother were still here, she wouldn't allow you to turn away from the only family you got!"

Yaz heard enough. It will not be a surprise to him if Aunt Margaret is in on the scheme, and he'd be damned if he listened to her besmirch his mother's name, as she always did when she lived.

"Aunt Margaret, I don't have time for this, when I'm ready to see Calvin I'll call him." Yaz pressed the end call button on his phone.

Yaz was ready to get over this phase of his life and it was time Jim and Calvin knew why he refused to meet with them. He scrubbed his hand down his face, and instantly his thoughts turned to Zoey. If it were not for Zoey and her busybody ways, he would have never known what Jim was doing to him.

Yaz reached for his phone and then paused. Three weeks had passed when last he saw or heard from Zoey. It annoyed him to admit he missed her with her bossy ways and sassy mouth, but he did. Yaz chuckled, as he scrolled down his contact list for her number.

In Duke's home gym, Zoey was on her last mile on the treadmill when the phone she had clipped to her side rang. "Hello," Zoey replied out of breath.

"Hi Sassy," Yaz spoke.

Surprised at hearing the familiar voice she both dreaded and secretly desired to hear, Zoey almost dropped the phone. She had to face the fact that she missed Yazair Bryant more than she cared to admit. Her heart jumped in her chest. "Hi," she said her voice sounding seductive breathless.

"How have you been Sassy?" Yaz replied.

Zoey rolled her eyes, but a smile lifted the corners of her mouth.

She liked the nickname he had given her when they worked together, although she would never let him know that.

"I'm fine, how about you?" She inquired.

"Things are better," Yaz replied.

"Good," she replied making small talk.

"Zoey, I wanted to thank you for helping me and making me aware of what's been going on behind my back."

"I was just trying to right a wrong," she said shyly.

Silence bounced between them. "You were right," Yaz stated.

"I know," she replied smugly, knowing he was speaking about Jim's embezzlement. "Have you fired Jim yet?"

"No not yet," he admitted. "Now the Duke Howard's firm represents me, he has offered to deal with everything for me, but I thought it best I confront Jim, plus I need to know why."

"Are you alright?" She asked forlornly. "I know it must be hard to find out someone you trusted all your life could betray you."

"Yeah it is, but it has to be done," Yaz exhaled in the phone.

"Um…, come to the meeting I'm having with Jim. Yaz voiced tentatively.

"You don't need me Yaz," she replied. As bad as she wanted to see that agent slash manager fall, she still declined.

"How would you feel if I told you, I just want you here?" Yaz countered.

Zoey heart hammered in her chest. This could be her reason to see Yaz again, she thought as her overactive brain chanted *Do It! Do It*!

"What time?" She asked defeated.

"In about an hour," Yaz replied.

"Okay, I'll be there, see you then."

"Thanks, Sassy," he replied grinning. That was easier than he thought.

Jim sat in the study of his five-bedroom, upscale home in Voorhees, NJ, wondering why for the past month that Yaz refused to see him without explanation. His instincts sensed that something was not right, and he still needed Yaz to sign the contracts that he had drawn up making him officially his manager/agent. If it were not for that holier than thou, David Singleton, he wouldn't have to go through all this trouble. Yaz was like a son to him; they did not need a contract. He was smart enough to have the contract claim that he owned Yazair Bryant, and the way his lawyer drew it up with all that legal mumbo jumbo, Yaz would never suspect a thing. There was no way in hell he was going to lose his cash cow over some stinking contract. The only difficulty he had now was Calvin and his greedy mother, Margaret. Somehow, they found out a couple of years ago that he was embezzling money from Yaz and threatened to tell Yaz if he didn't break them off a piece. He agreed and decided Calvin and his mother could be useful to him in the future, so he bent to their demands. Jim chuckled. Yaz has made him an extremely rich man, maybe not legally, but he was rich thanks to Yaz's trusting nature. He was tired of living in Yaz Bryant's shadow. If it were not for him, he would probably be in prison somewhere. Hell, the way he saw it, Yaz owed him. The first time he took a small amount of money from Yaz, but then when the big bucks started rolling in, so did his needs. It was a godsend when Yaz agreed to a power of attorney, now when he signed Yaz's name he felt no guilt at what he was doing. The $20 million will be the last, and if his luck held up Yaz would never find out, and once he paid

Calvin and Margaret off he would be smile all the way to the bank.

Jim walked into Yaz's home cocky as usual, with his briefcase in hand. Yaz swore under his breath. He was early and Zoey had not arrived yet.

"What the hell is going on with you? Since when did you avoid my calls and visits, man? I need to know what's going on with you at all times...,"

"Sit down Jim," Yaz interrupted coolly.

Jim stopped talking and frowned at Yaz. Something was going on, he could feel it, and it was not good. Jim's eyes narrowed on Yaz. What's going on?" He asked taking the offered seat placing his briefcase on the table between them.

Yaz sat on the sofa across from Jim and stared at his soon to be ex-manager.

"Am I late?" A familiar voice asked from the study door. Jim glared at the uninvited guest.

Yaz smiled and rose to greet his little tigress. "Hi Sassy," he greeted and kissed her cheek.

Zoey glanced at Yaz mildly surprised and suspicious of the kiss.

Jim looked between the two wondering what that bitch was doing here. Yaz took Zoey's hand leading her into the room. Was Yaz screwing her?

"Jim you remember Dr. Howard," Yaz introduced, as he led her to sit beside him on the sofa.

"I thought this was a business meeting, Yaz," Jim replied ignoring the introduction.

"Yes, it is," Yaz answered.

"Then why is she here?" Jim asked pointing a thick finger at her.

Still reeling from hurt and betrayal, Yaz looked at the man he once respected and love. Never would he have thought Jim would do this to him when for years he had trusted Jim with his life.

"Jim I want to see my financial portfolio, my contract with the Stallion and the endorsement deals you made on my behalf," he requested.

Jim eyes widened and then narrowed. "What do you need them for? You know I take care of you. The contracts are solid, and your finances are secured...," He paused. Jim slides to the edge of the chair to open his briefcase. " Yaz if you need something, whatever...,"

"No," he interrupted with dead calm. "I just want to see my financial portfolio, Jim."

Jim instantly became defensive. "What is it with you later, you don't trust me Yaz, after

43

all...?"

"All I want to see is my portfolio, Jim is there a problem?" Yaz asked his voice rising.

Zoey could see the situation was getting tense, and she still didn't know why she was here. Yaz steely gray eyes hardened and bore into Jim while his hands formed tight fists at his side, so tight Zoey could hear his knuckles cracking. Without thought, Zoey reached and gently caressed his right hand until it relaxed. Yaz glanced over at her, and he felt the tension leave his body. He now knew why he wanted her with him, she was his calming force, his muse. When he calmed, she removed her hand and demurely folded them in her lap. Jim did not miss that little exchange either.

"What's going on Yaz? Do you need to see Coco?" He asked with a sly chuckle. Zoey stiffened.

"Hell no, what does…," he took a deep calming breath. Look, Jim, I'm tired of this game. I know that you are ripping me off. I know Calvin and Aunt Margaret are probably involved too. The thing that hurts the most is that I trusted you more than I trusted any man on this earth. Disgusted Yaz came to his feet. "You're fired!"

Jim removed a handkerchief and wiped the sweat that broke out on Jim's face. How did he find out? Jim glared at Zoey, he knew that bitch had something to do with Yaz's accusations. Ever since that woman barged her way into Yaz life, he's changed.

"Yazy let me explain, I--I," Jim stuttered.

"How can you explain that you were ripping me off, Jim! You didn't give a damn about me, and all those damned endorsements you made me do while I was still hurt proved that while you procured the rewards, and I will deal with that later. What hurts the most was my contract with the Stallions was for $50 million dollars, you said it was $30 million. The Atlanta Bueto's offered 70 million when my contract was up…,"

"You were worth more…," Jim said quickly.

"No Jim, the fact is that they did not want to deal with you, at least, that's what the Bueto's managing staff told me when I talked to them."

Jim sputtered. "Yaz…,"

"Enough!" I want what you have stolen from me," He shouted.

"Yazy, come on man, we've been through too much together…,"

"So you're telling me you don't have $20 million plus of my money? Yaz growled.

44

"Of course, I do, I was looking out for your future and put some of the money aside. You have to understand Yaz you just got hurt I wasn't sure that you were going to recover so I started putting monies aside looking out for your future if you didn't recover enough to play football. You gotta believe me. I even had a contract drawn up between us so no one could take advantage of our relationship," Jim said frantically looking through his case for the papers.

Zoey remained quiet and watched as the drama unfolded. The man was now sweating profusely and he had to mop his forehead before his trembling hands dug into his briefcase. She knew he was lying and hoped Yaz didn't fall for his lame excuses.

"If all you say is true, why didn't you come to me? Why steal my money and then tell me I got less than what was signed for? I'll tell you why Jim because you were embezzling my money for your own future. There will be no contract between us; I've already signed with someone else."

Jim stood up sharply. "Who--who did you sign with?"

"Ellington Howard Consultants," Yaz stated. "I should have signed with him when he approached me in college, but I was too loyal to you, so I turned him down. Did you know he could have gotten me 100 million right out of college? I don't know how much you stole Jim, but I want my money back. And if, you don't give it back I will have you brought up on embezzlement charges. It's your call, Jim."

Jim knew it was over. He glared at the woman sitting on the couch. This was her fault. "What woke you up Yazy?" Jim sneered. "Don't tell me that bossy bitch got your nose wide and is leading you around by it?"

Zoey came to her feet. "Who are you calling a bitch, sleaze ball! You didn't give a rats butt about Yazair; you were in it for the money from the start of his career, and any fool could see that. Was it luck that he got injured or was it a setup?"

Jim had the nerve to look guilty.

"If I hadn't come when I did Yazair's career would have been over, you would have ruined him and taken his money without conscience. You are the worst kind man on this earth, a liar, and a thief."

Jim rushed at her with his hand raised. Yaz stepped in front of her. "Touch her and you die," he warned in a deadly calm tone. "If you ever call her out of her name again you will

45

spit teeth. Get out!!

Jim snatched up his case heading for the door.

"I expect those accounts before...," Yaz glanced at his watch, "five o'clock today, don't be one minute late or suffer the consequences. And tell Calvin to get a job and my Aunt to be happy with what she has; the Yazair National Bank is closed. Now get out of my house!"

Zoey could see Yaz was hurting. Quietly she moved behind him placing her hand on his back. Yaz turned, and she couldn't miss the hurt in his eyes, her heart went out to him.

"Yaz," she said softly and hugged him. Yaz arms wrapped tightly around her and he inhaled the sweet aroma that was all Zoey.

"I'm glad you came, thanks," his tone emotional.

Zoey lifted her head from his chest. Yaz eyes met hers.

"Why did you want me here? Zoey asked liking too much the feel of his arms around her.

Yaz kissed her forehead. "I wasn't sure at first, but now I know. When you touched my hand earlier, I felt a sense of calm come over me. That is when I knew Sassy you are my muse."

Zoey felt butterflies erupted in her belly and her breath seized in her chest. This was too much. She felt as if she were drowning in him.

"Oh please Yaz," she said pushing away needing to put a stop to the uncomfortable situation. "You think I'm going to fall for those player lines? You forget I have five brothers who swear they are all player's extraordinaire; I done heard um all, done heard um all," Zoey scoffed.

Yaz smiled inwardly. Sassy was scared. He heard her intake of breath and felt her heart racing rapidly when he held her. He affected her, and he knew it. A smile curled the corners of his mouth.

"Let me take you to dinner?" He countered.

Zoey frowned. "Why?"

Yaz grinned at her. "Because Zoey you are the only woman that keeps me calm."

Zoey gave an unladylike snort.

"Please give me a break with that player poetry," she replied backing away.

"So can I?" Yaz asked moving closer to her.

"Can you what?" Zoey asked staring at him. He was perfect, and his smile made her all soft and warm inside.

"Take you out." Yaz replied standing just a couple feet in front of her, and too close for comfort.

Her head fell back not wanting to lose contact with his sensual gray eyes.

Zoey stepped close. She realized she wanted him to kiss her again.

Yaz pulled her against him, his hand moving to caress the side of her neck. Her eyes shut as she allowed the heat of his touch to enthrall her. She gasped softly when she felt the tender touch of his lips on hers.

"Well, Sassy?" He whispered against her lips.

Warmth filled her stomach and those unfamiliar desires for him touch her. Her hand moved to his strong, well-formed chest, feeling his heat against the palm of her hands. When his mouth took her passionately, Zoey sank into the sensation.

Jim didn't hesitate to make it to the bank and transfer all Yaz's money back to his account. It left him only the money he earned from the percentage which would last him a while if he played it smart.

When the bank manager finished the transaction, he looked at Jim sternly.

"Mr. Bailey your accounts have been closed and we have written a check for the remaining balance," the back manager said sliding the check over to him. "We prefer to do business with honorable people, take your business elsewhere."

Snatching up the check Jim left the premises. So Yaz informed the Centennial Bank of misdeeds. He knew for facts that little bitch had something to do with this, and she would pay. Jim lifted his phone from the clip and furiously punched in the number. "Have your ass at my house in an hour!" He shouted.

Later while sitting in his study going over his assets, Jim Bailey roughly scrubbed his hand down his face. What was he going to do now that his meal ticket has flown the coop? He had a little money stashed away, but not enough to maintain the lifestyle he became accustomed to.

Jim's eyes slowly observed the room. He didn't want to put his 600 thousand dollar home as well as his condo in Center City on the market, but he had to start downsizing, and the house and condo were is largest assets. His restored deuce in a quarter caddy he couldn't bring himself to sell but the Escalade and Benz already had buyers. Jim dropped his head in his hand not sure what to do next.

He thought about the young and impressionable Yazair Bryant, who was fourteen when he and his mother Martha move to West Philly after her husband's sudden death, to live with her fraternal twin sister Margaret until Martha was able to find a job and a place to live. Martha Bryant was soft spoken, quiet, demure woman while Margaret was loud, obnoxious, and greedy when it came to the almighty dollar. It wasn't long before Martha landed a teaching position at the Overbrook High School, where he was the Phys Ed teacher and JV and Varsity football coach. He asked her on a date several times and each time she refused him. He had the feeling she didn't like or trust him. That didn't matter because she was too sedate for him. He met Yazair Bryant when he was a freshman at Overbrook High and went out for the junior varsity football team. At the age of fourteen, he was already six feet tall with a strong hard body and natural athletic skill. In all his years coaching football, he had never seen such raw talent in one so young. When the boy got his hands on the football and while running at top speed dodging tackles with precision and fluent grace, like poetry in motion. For a boy his size, you would expect to see some awkwardness; but not Yaz. Right away he knew with his talent and with his help and guidance Yazair Bryant would go far. At first, Martha was against the whole idea of her son playing football and she voiced her concerns about her son being an athlete. Her feelings were that he was too intelligent to waste his mind on football with the possibility of getting severely injured. Yet, Yaz really wanted to play and his mother allowed it with a few stipulations of her own, and that was if his grade fell, he could forget about playing football.

Yaz not only played football well but kept his GPA at 4.0 all four years at Overbrook. Upon graduation, the college football scouts were on Yaz-like white on rice. He had offers from Notre Dame, Ole Miss, and many other All-American College. Yaz opted to attend Penn State on a full academic scholarship so he could stay home with his mother.

Yaz overall was a good kid, that is until he got in trouble while hanging out with his cousin Calvin, who had been caught shoplifting. Calvin blamed everything on Yaz, and when it was all said and done, Calvin was the one stealing. Calvin was rotten to the core and was proud to be.

Jim saw the big picture as far as Yaz's career was concerned and elected to make Yaz his primary project. He did everything he could to see that he was a success because if Yaz were a success, he would be a success and the boy didn't fail him. Not only did the boy excel academically, but he was also named MVP all four years at Penn State and then to the championship, earning him the Heisman Trophy.

He earned Yaz trust and respect becoming his career manager and Jim knew that his life was going to bring him financial freedom as long has he had Yaz in the palm of his hand. Jim's thoughts shifted to the confrontation he had with Martha Bryant. Yaz was weeks away from his graduation when Martha confronted him with her suspicions. The demure and quiet Martha was lioness when it came to her son and his well-being.

How she found out that he accepted illegal enticements from some of the colleges that wanted to enroll Yaz into their universities were beyond him, but Martha got word of it and one day barged into his office.

"I knew you were sleazy Jim from the first day I met you," she exclaimed angrily. *"How dare you put my son's life and future in jeopardy and then implicate me in your little scheme."*

"Calm down Martha, what are you talking about?"

Martha's face heated with anger. "I received a letter from some college down South informing me the $20,000 had to be returned because Yaz didn't choose their college like you promised them. What did you do? You knew Yaz had already accepted the full scholarship from Penn State."

"Martha let me explain. Yaz was supposed to give Penn State two years and then transfer to the college down south. It was all on the up and up. Next year Yaz is going to transfer," he stated.

"Yaz is not transferring anywhere. He will graduate from Penn State, and you are going to return that money to those people, and then I want you to stay away from my son, or I will call the college myself and expose you and anyone else that tries to take advantage of my son.   Fortunately, Yaz never found out and then tragically, right after Yaz graduated, Martha was a victim of a random mugging and was killed. After his mother's death, Yaz didn't care what happened to him. He started drinking excessively and partying heavily. His ego was boundless, and Jim nurtured it to his advantage. Eventually, Yaz turned everything over to him to manage, and he knew that everything would be to his advantage.

Everything was falling into place until that nosy ass therapist interfered into Yaz life, and she had to be dealt with immediately. He could not prove it, but he knew Yaz was involved with the bitch. He had heard from others that they were often seen together. She definitely had to be shut down before Yaz did something stupid and married the girl.

Pulling out his phone, he punched out a number. "I need a favor. I want you to watch someone for me, and there's five hundred dollars in for you, and don't mess this up like you did the last time. Follow her and let me know where she goes and what she does," Jim ordered. After giving him what info he had on Zoey, he hung up and punched out another number. "Hello Trish," Jim greeted.

Dazed Zoey hopped into her VW punch buggy and went home. She was in trouble on many levels. First, she agreed to go on a date with Yaz, second her brothers were going to kill her and third, she didn't have anything to wear or where to begin to dress up for a date. It's not like she did not love clothes and shopping, she only purchased comfortable clothes that pertained to her work. She did own a pair of five-inch heels she sometimes wore to strut around her apartment and was darned good at it and she would be the first to tell anyone she knew nothing about fashion. She was raised by five brothers and her father when her mother died giving birth to her. All she knew was sports. Although Dad had hired Miss Thelma as her nanny who came every day to dress her, combed her hair for school and tried to teach her how to be a young lady, it was after a few weeks that Miss Thelma quit because she said she could not manage a little girl that was just as ornery, mischievous and rough as her brothers.

Now she had problems because she didn't own a dress, never did, and she certainly didn't have any evening wear since she never went out so she didn't see the sense in it. She always wore her hair in a ponytail most of the time and she didn't wear makeup. She was doomed. She really wanted to go out with Yaz, because she found she liked their verbal sparring and she especially enjoyed kissing him. She was soon to be twenty-six, and she never had a man show her the attention, but Yaz did. Other men she knew saw her as a little sister or just one of the guys because of her interests in sports along with her profession. Zoey sighed loudly. "What you gonna do girl?" She asked aloud. A smile brightened her face and one name popped to head, Caitlin Smith. That was what she could do. She could call her best friend.

Zoey met Cat when they attended Temple University. Cat was eight years older and her best friend and former roommate when they attended Temple U. Cat was a marketing and public relations major from Newark, NJ. Cat was a few inches taller than her five feet four-inch height, with silky curly dark brown hair that fell below the middle of her back. Her caramel complexion was flawless, and her features were small and dainty. Cat was beautiful, feminine, feisty, and Zoey loved her, but Duke didn't like her at all. The one summer break from school she bought Cat home one Duke rudely began questioning her person life, and Cat left but not before telling her older brother off. After that had blown over, Cat visited often, most times ignoring Duke and enjoyed her the time they spent together anyway. All Duke and Cat did was disagree about everything anyway. Cat constantly called him Ellington, and Duke thought Cat was too old for her to associate with. It didn't take much to get a disagreement started and Zoey learned to leave them at it. After graduation, Cat found a job with a marketing firm in New York where she now lived. She now is the head of her department with a fabulous corner office. It has been a few weeks since she has spoken to her and with Cat's high profile job and her practice they hardly had time to visit. Even though, they were best friends, she didn't know much about Cat. Her private life has been just that, private. She would call Cat, tell her the dilemma, and beg for her help if she had too. Her next problem is telling her brothers she was going on a date with a professional athlete. They had told her when she was a teenager, dating athletes are forbidden to their little sister. They had nothing against her dating, just dating athletes would not be tolerated, especially football and basketball players. She didn't care what the rules were, she wanted to go out with Yaz and her brothers were not going to stop her. She was twenty-five for goodness sakes.

When she was still in high school, some of the boys showed an interest in her one day, and then the next day they avoided her like she had the cooties and she didn't understand why. Later she found out her brothers were threatening them and she didn't speak to them for almost a month. When they promised to stop intimidating the boys interested in her, it was too late, the damage was already done. Not one of the boys in her classes ever talked to her again. She wasn't even invited to the prom, so she pretended it did not matter, but deep down it hurt her. She never told her brothers how much.

She called Cat, and without pause, she agreed to help her and would arrive in Cherry Hill early Friday morning. The first thing Cat asked was *"Does the Neanderthal know?"* When she told Cat he didn't, she suggested that she not tell him, let him find out the night Yaz picked her up. Cat was right. If her brothers knew they would do all they could to stop her from going out with Yaz.

Chapter Six

Yaz sat at the board table with Duke, Cab, Dizzy, and Satch. He didn't realize it was such a process to be affiliated with the popular marketing team and was surprised to see the football, hockey and basketball player they represted and each one were superstars and pillars of their communities. The brothers encouraged their clients to use their educations to have off-season careers. They also stressed that they had no problem with partying, but they did have a problem with overindulgence, and if any of their clients didn't follow the Howard Rules was first warned and then dropped. He knew that most professional athletes fell all over themselves to get representation from the Howard Brothers because they genuinely cared about their clients and had knack for getting them the best endorsement and contracts.

The first rule of the establishment is to respect yourself and others. Second, large egos are frowned upon and will be personally exercised by the brothers. Third Rule: The door is always open, and the fourth rule is we got your back. All the brothers expected honesty, integrity, truth and be self-confident, but humble in all they do. No one player was bigger than the other was and everyone got equal and fair time with his agents. They had a strict punishment system. If you missed practice without a valid reason for doing so, not only did the team issue fines, the brothers did as well. Anyone that did not want to work for the greater good was shown the door, and everyone in the profession knew Ellington 'Duke' Howard's clientele because of the way these athletes behaved.

Yaz being newly on board and with his rep of being egotistical had to prove himself worthy of their representation. Everyone knew he was one of the best running back in the league and could have gotten top dollar with strong representation, and he was determined to make a favorable impression on the Howard brothers for two reasons. The first reason he had something to prove to the brothers, and he wanted to erase the rep he created of himself and the second was their little sister.

Duke was his representing agent for now until he proved himself, although all the brothers had a say in a client's best interest. Cab took the management of his funds while Satch would make him marketable. Quarterly you sat down with Cab as he discussed your financial portfolio. He was there to advise you on any investments you wanted to make and if it was a good move for the individual. You were still responsible for your own money, so if you were frivolous with your finances, it was on you. During the interview, he had to do a personality questionnaire, so the company had some knowledge of his likes and dislikes. Sitting at the table with these four impregnable men that pulled his card and listed all the bad choices he made in his career so far had him fuming, but he knew he was wrong and deserved the chastisement. So that he had something to keep him busy during the off-season, Dizzy obtained an interview for an entry-level engineering position, but it was up to him to present himself and be awarded the position of the firm.

Yaz talked with some of the other players in the league he knew was represented by the brothers liked them and appreciated their care while others hated them. However, the others that used to be part of Howard Consultants, and didn't want to abide by the Howard Creed as it was known wished they had. Once you were dismissed, you were not welcomed back. All Yaz knew he was ready for that fresh, wholesome life his Momma wanted for him.

Weeks after he fired Jim he tried again to talk to him as well as his cousin and aunt. As far as he was concerned, he was done with them. It hurts that the only family he had cared so little for him, but cared more about what he could give them.

"Don't you dare cut your hair Zo," Cat yelled at her.

"Cat my hair needs cutting, everybody cannot have those silky curls like yours," Zoey pouted.

"Let me tell you something, I must surely be mixed with something, she giggled. Zoey smiled at her friend. "With that beautiful dress and the makeover, Yazair Bryant is not going to recognize you that I promise, and he's not going to want to let you go either.

Zoey looked at Cat hopeful. She wanted to be beautiful, not just for him, but for herself. Yaz was the prom she missed.

Zoey had cleared her appointments for the day as she waited for Cat's arrival early that morning, and they have been at it all day. They hit Philly's exclusive boutiques and when they were done, Zoey had everything from the finest underwear to the latest style in clothes and shoes. The makeover she was now getting proved how beautiful Zola Howard truly is. Her long, thick wavy hair was now smooth and silky to her shoulders, and the stylist taught her how to apply her makeup to enhance her natural beauty.

Cat smiled at her friend. Not only was she going to knock that fine Yazair Bryant for a loop, but her well-meaning, overprotective brothers will be doing a little looping themselves.

It was time they let Zo have a life. She was not the fragile flower her brothers seem to think she was. Cat chuckled. She witnessed firsthand when that little girl's mother of a right hook had knocked someone on their butt in the middle of the cafeteria when they attended Temple U.   Although she hated the way her brothers smothered her, she also envied the love they had for their little sister. She wished she had someone to love and care for her as her brothers did Zo. She doubted she would ever know what real love and caring are about with her dysfunctional past. So, she decided early in life she was never going to let anyone get close enough to show her what love was about. She probably would remember it anyway.

Cat trusted no one, but Zoey. Oh, how she wished she could open up to the one person she trusted, but was afraid if she knew the truth about her she would lose the only real friend she had if she revealed she had no past. Yet still even after eighteen years that time in her life sometimes came back to her enveloping her in the darkness that was once her life. She didn't want to go back there, but sometimes things would trigger a memory, and there she was again fighting for her life and sanity living a daytime nightmare. Cat blinked her eyes rapidly to ease the sting of the tears that gathered behind them.

"Cat! Cat!" Zoey called concerned.

Cat turned to her friend. "Oh my God, you are beautiful Zo, I always said so," she grinned.

Zoey was not fooled. Something was bothering Cat, however with her head focused on her first date, she decided to let it go now, but she vowed she will badger her later.

Zoey smiled. "You think Yaz will notice?"

"Girl he is going to flip and Ellington is going to have a conniption." Cat clapped her hands excitedly. "I can't wait."

Zoey shook her head, round two of Duke and Cat.

Friday nights were usually Family Night for the Howard's. They order take-out, played games, and watched movies and simply bonded. This Friday was unusual because Jelly could join his family, which was not often during basketball season.

"Where's Zoey? Jelly asked. "I ordered her favorite nachos and wings."

"Yeah where is Little Bit?" Cab asked clicking the remote to the 52" flat screen.

Duke went to the intercom system. "Come on Zo, were ready to eat," he ordered.

"Since when do the five of you wait for me to eat?" Zoey replied. Cat covered her mouth to quiet her giggle.

"Just hurry Pud," Duke said clicking off.

"You look amazing," Cat commented.

Zoey smiled her thanks. Yaz refuse to tell her where they were going, said he wanted to surprise her. So she decided to wear the black cocktail dress simple in design. The front had a modest scoop neck, but the back dipped to her waist and fit her curvaceous body perfectly and four-inch black strapped sandal covered her dainty feet. Her only accessories were a pair of diamond, onyx studded earrings with a matching bracelet, and a black silk shawl with gold woven into the fabric. Her hair was loosely curled falling just below her shoulders. Her makeup was fierce, her hair was fierce, and her dress was fierce. Zoey stared at herself in the full-length mirror, she felt a little bare in the dress, but she knew she looked and felt special. "He should be here soon," she smiled nervously at Cat.

The brothers were having a heated debate over the players that would make the All-Star Playoff for the NBA when the doorbell rang.

"Your clients are not the only players in the NBA," Jelly teased rising to answer the door.

"Yeah, but they are the best," Duke called after him. "Are you expecting someone?" He asked his other brothers. They shook their heads.

"Someone go and get Zo, I'm hungry," Cab complained.

Jelly returned followed by an extremely well-dressed Yazair Bryant. The brother looked terrific.

"Hey, Yaz, what brings you here all decked out?" Duke asked rising to shake his hand.

"I have a date," he announced.

"Really, anyone we know?" Satch asked.

"Yes, Zola Howard," he answered smiling.

The room instantly quieted. Each brother's eyes turned to him and the friendly greeting he received when he first arrived had changed to hard cold glares. Each brother slowly came to their feet.

"Zola!" Duke roared without the use of the intercom as he continued to glower at Yaz.

Zoey stood in the doorway of the den with a demure smile on her pretty face. Each brother and Yaz turned when they heard her enter the room and their mouths dropped open at the sight of their baby sister looking very beautiful and sexy.

Yaz always thought she was pretty, but this Zoey was exquisite.

When the brothers finally came to their senses, and the initial shock was gone, each one shouted "Hell no!"

Cat then stepped in front of Zoey and glared at each brother.

"Where in the hell did she come from?" Duke shouted and turned his stony face in Cat's direction.

Cat approached Duke and glared up at him. "Don't you dare ruin this for her Ellington, I swear I'll cut you," she threatened.

Duke's mouth dropped open. "You heard that? I told you, she was too old to be hanging with Zoey, she is a bad influence!"

"Oh do be quiet Ellington," Cat replied.

Yaz and Zoey watched as the drama began to unfold. He was in shock and could not pull his eyes from her while she listened to her brothers going back and forth.

"She cannot go out with him, she knows the rules!"

"That dress is too tight!"

"It's too short!"

"What did she do to her hair?"

"Does she have on makeup?"

Zoey listened to her brother's and felt like she was on display and awaiting their judgment. Cat looked over at Zoey and saw tears shining in her eyes. Zoey glanced at her and swiftly left the room the echo of her heels on the marble floors in her wake.

Cat put her fingers to her lips and gave a loud shrilled whistle and then punched Duke in his chest. Duke hand went to the injured spot and frowned down at her.

"You are all the most insensitive jackasses I've ever met. This night meant so much to Zoey, and not one of you had the decency to tell her how beautiful she looks. All you cretins did is complain about her dress too tight and short and what happened to her hair she mocked. "Jackasses!" Cat spat.

"That's the problem, she looks too beautiful. And, what in the hell are you doing asking our baby out?" Duke growled at Yaz.

"Zo is a twenty-five year old woman if you haven't noticed. She deserves to have a life, you morons. I know the five of you have your hoochie's, well Zoey deserves to have a social life too, and the five of you are sucking the life out of her."

The brothers did have the decency to drop their heads sheepishly. Cat addressed Yaz. "I told her, she should have had you pick her up at her door. But no, she wanted the Moron Five to see how good she looks. Please Yazair don't leave, give her a minute, she wanted this so much." Cat had said before she turned to leave.

"Yaz looked directly in Duke's eyes. "I'm not going anywhere," he stated confidently. Each brother glared at him, but neither said anything.

After Cat had gone, Jelly was the first to speak. "Damn she's bossy," he muttered.

Satch grinned. "I like her, is she single?"

"Touch her Satch, and your ass is mine!" Duke threatened.

"But you hate her Duke," Cab replied confused. "You said....,"

"Stay away from her!" Duke bellowed.

"What about Victoria?" Satch asked.

"That's right. Vicky thinks you gonna jump de broom," Jelly teased, and the other brothers snicker even Yaz mouth twitched.

"Victoria knows where we stand, and anyway we've only been out a few times," Duke stated dismissively.

"A girl can hope, and you know that you are not getting any younger," Cab drawled.

"You're a year younger than I am Cab; if I'm old what are you?" He argued.

"Younger than you," Cab replied cockily.

"He's got a point," Jelly the younger brother started laughing.

"Why are we arguing?" Dizzy interjected. "Yaz here is taking our baby out and he needs to know the rules!"

"Sit down Yaz," Duke ordered.

Before Duke could speak, they heard the women returning. "Disrespect her and you die," Duke whispered. "Smile," he ordered his brothers.

Cat stood behind Zoey as she reentered the room, and raised her fist at each brother in warning.

"You are beautiful Sassy," Yaz complimented.

"Sassy," the brothers mouthed to each other.

"Yes, Pud, you look beautiful," Duke added sincerely.

"Thank you brothers, I love you," she replied.

"We love you too," they chorused.

Zoey turned to Yaz and smiled. "Ready?" Just as she walked past her brother's the shawl that was draped over her her shoulders slid to the floor displaying her bare curved back. An audible gasp was heard throughout the room and Cat glared at each brother in turn. Zoey never noticed the shawl had slipped off and Yaz approached her and lifted the shawl from the floor. When he saw what the brother gasped about, he looked at each one and swallow seeing the warning in their eyes. Without touching her, Yaz replaced the shawl on her shoulders. Smiling sweetly, Zoey thanked him and moved towards the door. Cat grinned. "Get it, Girl," she whispered walking them to the door.

When the door closed all hell broke loose. Four of the five brothers rushed to the door, but Cat stepped in front of the door blocking it. Duke followed at a slower pace still stunned at his baby sister. When did she grow up and when did she become such a beautiful woman he wondered.

Duke stood and watched as Cat barred the door.

"You morons are not going to follow and embarrass her," Cat scolded folding her arms across her chest stubbornly.

"We won't embarrass her; we just want to make sure Yaz keeps his hands where they belong, that is all." Satch calmly explained.

Cat shook her head. "You will have to go through me first."

"Please, little girl, I can lift you with one hand," Satch boasted.

"Try it," Cat challenged. "Plus you don't know where they are going, and I do," she bluffed grinning.

Satch took a step toward Cat.

"Don't try it," Duke warned Satch.

"We're just gonna tie her up until she tells us where, Little Bit is going," Satch reasoned.

"Leave Pud alone," Duke ordered and returned to the den.

Each brother looked at each other confused. "Did Duke forget the no athletes rules?" Jelly asked scratching his head.

Cat chuckled. "You idiots, Ellington realizes Zo is a grown woman and it times to cut the apron strings already," she laughed. "Now, come on buttheads, I'll beat you all in monopoly," Cat challenged slipping her arm through Satch and Cab. "If I lose I will make the best breakfast brunch you have ever had." Jelly and Dizzy followed the trio.

They all looked so pitiful when the realization that their baby has grown up, and knowing they had to come to terms with it.

"She's beautiful just like Mom," Dizzy commented.

Chapter Seven

The June breeze lifted her silky hair from her shoulders. In the circle driveway, Zoey couldn't help noticing the silver Corvette she knew didn't belong to any of her brothers. Zoey glanced at Yaz. "Nice car," she complimented.

Thanks," he replied grinning as he opened the door. Zoey sat in the low-slung car and swung her leg inside. After he had closed the door, Zoey heart fluttered as her eyes followed his swagger around to the driver's side. Yaz slide into the car press a button on his keys and the engine purred; he put the car in gear drove out of the driveway. Zoey took a quick look at him. Yaz Bryant is a good-looking man and he looked extremely handsome in his navy Armani suit. Yaz eyes met hers.

"You take my breath away Sassy," he said smoothly stopped in the driveway. He reached over and lifted her hand to his lips. With her hand still in his, he pulled onto the highway that would take them to his surprise date. Zoey inhaled deeply gazing at his profile.

"Your scent intoxicates me, baby. I could find you just by your scent in a crowded room.

They say that is how the male species knows their mates." He replied smiling.

"Are you my mate Sassy?"

"Are we animals Mr. Bryant?" Zoey smiled at him.

Yaz chuckled.

"Where are you taking me?" She asked as she eased her hand from his. If he continued to hold it, her heart would leap clear from her chest.

"You'll see," he grinned.

Zoey head rested on the headrest and closed her eyes, enveloped in the sultry sound of the soft jazz playing, along with Yaz's sensual scent and the exhilaration of her heart was taking her to a place she never thought she would ever go. She smiled. This was her prom.

"Your prom?" Yaz repeated smiling.

"Did I say that out loud?" She asked sheepishly shyly glancing at him.

Yaz nodded. "Explain please."

"In high school, any boy interested in me my brother scared away. Word got around that the Howard boys would hurt any boy that talked to their sister. So, I did not get to go the prom because the guy's in my class were afraid to ask. So prom night I stayed in my room and cried all night. I didn't speak to them for about a month."

Yaz felt awful for her, but he understood why. If she were his sister, he would keep the boys away too.

"You said you dated a little, how did they handle that?"

"I lied," she stated.

"You've never dated?" Yaz asked stunned. Zoey was beautiful; he thought for sure she was turning them away in droves.

"If you count the people you work with, then yes I've dated."

"If you were my sister and look the way you do tonight, I'd have to hurt someone too," he stated smiling.

"But you are not my brother," Zoey replied sultrily.

"Are you flirting with me," Yaz asked in kind.

Zoey chuckled softly. "I think I am. I didn't think I knew how," she giggled. "I think I like flirting, and I'm going to do it more often," she started feeling confident.

Arriving at their destination, Yaz parked the car, turned off the engine, turned slowly towards her. Zoey looked out the window awed. They were at Penn's Landing, and the docked Spirit of Philadelphia was boarding several couples dressed in their finery into the elegant ship. Smiling and pleasantly surprised, Zoey turned to him.

Slowly in that sexy baritone voice, Yaz enlightened her.

"The only, flirting you will be doing is with me and only me."

"Really?" Zoey whispered gazing into his seductive gray eyes.

"Yes."

Their lips met, and their tongues danced seductively. Zoey purred when Yaz's fingers slipped through her silky locks bringing her closer thoroughly tasting her. Slowly they parted, but stay close.

"Shall we go?" Yaz asked against her lips, his warm minty breath tantalizing her libido.

"Mm...," was the only reply she could make.

"Sassy if we don't board now, we won't be."

"Oh--oh, I'm ready," she replied.

Yaz gave her a light kiss on the lips before getting out of the car.

Even though, it was warm, Zoey had the shawl around her shoulder concealing her beautiful bare back. It was a good thing Yaz thought. If he caught any man admiring with lust, he would be dotting several eyes tonight. Although he was proud to have this beautiful woman on his arm, he would not tolerate any man eyeing her delectable body. All eyes were on the handsome couple as they were escorted to their private table. Zoey did not miss the many eyes watching as they moved through the ship's dining room; she was sure all eyes were on the handsome running back. When it circulated who he is, several people stopped by their table, and he graciously talked to the Philadelphia fans.

"Tell you what; after I feed this extremely beautiful lady, we will meet you in the nightclub so we don't disturb the other people trying to enjoy their dinner." They left satisfied.

The table was perfect. They sat were the full moon seem to shine only on them. Zoey especially like the way it reflected on the water. The server assigned to their table came with menus. Everything on the menu made Zoey's mouth water. She looked over the top of the menu at Yaz smiling. "Don't let this petite body fool you. I'm not one of those salad eating and lemon water drinking chicks," she informed looking again at the menu. Yaz chuckled shaking his head.

The food was delicious, and a silence settled around the stuffed couple. The shawl that was draped around Zoey's shoulders now lay over the back of her chair, and she rested her chin on her fist a satisfied smile on her perfect lips. Yaz smiled at the satisfied beauty sitting across from him.

"Yaz have you heard from Jim or your family?" She didn't miss the muscle tick in his jaw. "I'm sorry--I...,"

"No it's okay," he assured her. "Calvin and my aunt came to the house telling me, they knew Jim was cheating me. Jim claims they blackmailed him into giving them money to keep silent. It was a mess, just a bunch of finger pointing and lies. Aunt Margaret then tried the guilt trip and family blood bull. She had the nerve to say my mother expected me to take care of her and Calvin."

"What? You're kidding?"

"Unbelievable, right? My mother and Aunt Margaret were twins, but not identical. For some reason, my aunt didn't care too much for my mother. Even after she died my aunt never had a kind thing to say about her. I may be biased, but my mother was a saint. Never said an unkind word about or to anyone, except for Jim; I never understood why she disliked him so much… guess I know now, huh," he said dejectedly.

You miss her a lot don't you? Zoey asked compassionately. She noticed the sheen of tears in his eyes and was sorry she brought it up. Her mother had her late in life and died giving birth to her, so she didn't know her, but she did have her five brothers and Dad. At the age of five, her father died from prostate cancer and she understood how devastated he must have been to lose his mother. The sad thing is Yaz had two conniving relatives that thought he owed them something.

"Yes, I miss her very much...," He paused. "Zoey my mother didn't die of some illness; she was murdered by a mugger."

Zoey hand covered her heart, and she gasped. "Oh Yaz I'm so sorry I brought this up, please...,"

Yaz reached over and covered her hand. "It's okay. I never talked about her with anyone until you; it always hurt too much. When she died..." He paused. I don't know, it seemed I had nothing left. "I'm just glad she saw me, when I graduated, and when I received the

Heisman Trophy, but she never got to see me play pro ball." Yaz chuckled. "She was my biggest fan and kept me grounded. She didn't miss any of my games from high school to college and the one thing I do know she was proud of me, and that makes me feel better. That is why before each game, I always blow her a kiss because I know she is there in my heart and spirit."

Zoey smiled. She had noticed before every game he would run out to the center of the field, press his fingers to his lips and lift them to the sky. The fans would go crazy. She thought he was arrogant and was flirting with his many groupies.

"David said you changed after your mother passed."

Yaz frowned. "When did he tell you that?"

Zoey grinned. "When he persuaded me to take you back as a patient after I quit."

Yaz chuckled. "I fired you," he stated and smiled.

"How can you fire someone if you did not hire them?" She argued.

"You got me there, but you came back. Why?"

Zoey pulled her hand from beneath his and looked out at the city lights twinkling from the ship. She didn't want to answer him. Even then, she felt an attraction to him. But it was more than an attraction, and she didn't want to entertain the fact that she was falling for him.

"Why Sassy?" He repeated. She turned her attention back to him.

"Because I believe underneath all that rancor and arrogance is a good man," she stated truthfully.

Yaz did not expect that and was humbled by her response. He came around the table, "Come let's go dancing," he said extending his hand.

Zoey gazed up at him marveling at how gorgeous Yaz Bryant was.

His brows rose. "Don't tell me, you can't dance?" He challenged.

"I dance better than Michael Jackson," she boasted placing her hand in his.

At their arrival to the nightclub, a cheer went up. There was live entertainment, but the band was taking a break, and a tremendously talented DJ was jamming. Yaz sat Zoey at an empty table and went to greet some of the fans as he promised. She frowned. "Oh no, he didn't just leave her sitting alone." Zoey tossed her shawl on the chair, and moved through the group of men talking to Yaz and continued to the dance floor. Yaz mouth dropped open as she moved gracefully passed him. He watched as every man's eyes in the group followed the sexy, petite woman.

"Oh hell no," he growled when the group left him and followed Zoey to the dance floor. Weaving his way to her side, he kept his eyes on her delectable body swaying and moving with style and grace while she danced between two men. He paused shortly and watched until one of her dance partners reached out to touch her. Swiftly he was on the dance floor twirling her into his. "Mine!" He growled to the startled partner.

"Jealous much?" She grinned up at him only mildly surprised when he expertly maneuvered her into his arms.

"Jealous much about you," he stated confidently.

She was pressed firmly against him when the tempo of the music changed to a slow, seductive number. An excellent dancer Yaz led Zoey expertly and effortlessly on the dance floor, and she could have stayed in his arms forever. She raised her head, looked into the radiant gray of his eyes, and was lost. His head lowered, and Zoey caught up in the moment offered her lips. His mouth covered hers; skillfully he took control tasting her sweetness. A bright light flashed in her head. She was falling in love with Yazair Bryant, and boy was she in trouble.

As the night wore on, they danced together and with others, with the men's understanding they were not allowed to touch. The live entertainment returned and started their set with a provocative reggae number. Zoey smiled seductively at Yaz and began to gyrate to the stimulating beats, moving as if she were a born and bred island girl. Zoey danced tantalizingly dazzling him. Several women pulled their partners on the dance floor mimicking Zoey's moves, not quite as well, but they had their men's attention. Yaz grasped her waist pulling her shapely gyrating bottom into a semi hard erection she caused. She felt it because her hips swaying against it.

"You're killing me," he leaned and whispered in her ear.

Zoey looked brazenly over her shoulder into his smoldering eyes. "Then take me out of here," she whispered back.

Yaz pulled her from the dance floor, grabbed her shawl and had her buckled in his Corvette.

Cat had retired to bed about eleven o'clock after his brother's left leaving Ellington in the den watching ESPN. It was now after one and Zoey still had not returned. They all wanted to stay and wait for Zo, but Ellington reminded them Zoey was a grown woman and kicked them out. Cat moved through the large house from Zo private rooms to the den and stood in the doorway. Ellington large body sprawled out on the sofa no doubt waiting for his sister. Cat shook her head as she watched him. If he wasn't such a stuck up and prudish, he would be a remarkably handsome man. Hell, who was she trying to fool? Ellington Howard was fine. Too bad, she was not available. She quietly studied him; the perfectly neat trimmed beard that outlined his strong jaw line putting an emphasis on his sensual, full mouth. That hooked nose that boasted of the Native American in his blood and long, thick lashes that rested on his cheekbones. Ellington was delicious; too bad his disposition didn't match his outer package. From the moment, they met six years ago they were at each other's throats. If he thought he could bully her, he got a rude awakening. She had to stand up and fight all her life, and Gigantor was not going to intimidate her.

Grabbing a throw cover from the chair, she spread it over him. Just when she turned to leave, he grabbed her hand pulling her down on him. Panic immediately evaded her, taking her back to a time in her life that still haunted her. Violently she struggled against him, her arms and legs flailing wildly.

"Cat! Cat!" he shouted her name trying to subdue her.

"No! No! Please, don't hurt me anymore," she cried frantically. Duke released her. She fell to the floor and scrambled away from him; her face pale beneath her coppery coloring, her dark eyes wild with terror. Cat turned to flee. Concerned Duke caught her around her waist pulling her back into his chest.

"No! No! No!" She screamed as her nails cut into his arm however Duke ignored the pain only wanting to calm and reassure her he would never hurt her.

"Cat, sh--sh, I would never hurt you," he said gently in her ear.

Duke rocked her while he softly talked. "It's alright sweetheart, I would never hurt you. I will protect you with my life always." Gradually the tension eased. He lifted her in his arms, and she curled into his chest her arms tightly around his neck. Duke sat down cradling, rocking her as she sobbed until only whimpers were heard, and the soft sound of her breathing as she slept. Still cradling his arm, Duke's heart slowly returned to normal as he gazed into her sleeping face, gently wiping tears that clung to her face.

"What happened to you, sweetheart?" He whispered.

After holding her a long while, Duke rose with her in his arms and put her to bed in the guest room in Zoey's apartment. He switched off the light. Suddenly she sat up.

"Ellington please don't leave me." Silently, Duke lay down and spooned her into his body. Before Cat's eyes closed, she realized this was the closest she has allowed any man, and why did he make her feel so protected and safe?

Yaz and Zoey rode in silence. When he left the ship, he had every intention of taking her to his house and make love to her; and she wanted it. He could smell her arousal blended with her sensual fragrance. He had the feeling Zoey's never been with a man, and he wanted to be her first and last, but not like this. It had to be special, something neither would forget. Twenty minutes later, they were pulling into her private driveway. Zoey glanced at him confused. She thought for sure Yaz wanted her. So why did he take her home?

He turned off the engine and turned to her. Gently he cupped her cheek, tracing her lower lip with his thumb.

"I want you Sassy, more than you know, but I also want our first time to be special," he told her.

Yes, Zoey thought dreamily, I love this man. She smiled. "Come by for brunch and we can work out together. Duke has a state of the art equipment room," she invited not wanting to miss a single day without seeing him.

Yaz inwardly grimaced. He did not want to sit and be glared at by her five brothers. "How about I take you to brunch, and then we can go to Hershey Park?" He suggested returning her smile.

She giggled. "How about you pick me up at eleven o'clock?"

At her door Zoey thanked him for a wonderful night and before entering her apartment, Yaz kissed her so thoroughly she was sure she would never get to sleep. She sighed loudly and leaned against the door. She wanted to talk about her evening. Kicking off her shoes, she knocked softly on Cat's door before she opened it. Cat was out like a light. Quietly closing the door went to her room undressed and was asleep before her head hit the pillow with a serene smile on her face.

Chapter Eight

Duke sat up frowning and glanced at his bedside clock. The most incredible aroma assaulted his senses and filled his room. The housekeeper was off on Saturday and Zoey never got up this early on the weekend. Caitlin Smith.

Duke jumped out of the bed, showered, slipped on a pair of jeans and T-shirt and followed the awesome aromas. He had not smelled that kind of food since his Momma passed twenty-five years ago. He slowed when he passed the dining room and the double table was set in a buffet style. The center of the table decorated with a fresh assortment of flowers, with plates, silverware, and his stainless steel chafing dishes he bought three years ago and never used. He had not forgotten the feel of Cat in his arms because he stayed spooned with her until she fell into a deep slumber. What he forgot is her promise to his greedy brothers that she would prepare a buffet for them if they beat her at monopoly that they began cheating on the first toss of the dice.

He continued on to his state of the art kitchen that he barely used. He stood in the doorway of the brightly lit space. His heart flipped, and a knot formed in his stomach at the sight of Cat bent over the oven in shorts that displayed her well-endowed shapely bottom. Nice was not the word he would use to describe the view. Not wanting to spook her, he spoke.

"Mornin'."

Cat turned her mitt cover hands holding two pans of hot golden biscuits. She smiled. Morning Ellington," she greeted placing the pan of biscuits on the towel cover counter. "There's coffee brewing."

"Thanks. Wow, you've been busy," he said looking over the kitchen where she had already prepared several dishes. Can I help with something?" He offered.

"Yes, care to make pancake batter?" She asked.

Duke shrugged. "Yeah, if you show me how."

"Use that bowl, there," she pointed, "and then get the pancake flour, eggs, milk, and vanilla." Cat watched as Ellington got what she asked.

Curious she asked. "You have a kitchen with everything a chef could want and you don't use the stuff, why?"

"I can't cook," Duke admitted sheepishly. "Nevertheless, I try. So I thought if I had a kitchen that had everything, I would learn."

Cat chuckled. "Well, you are going to make pancakes today, because your brothers will be here in about an hour, so let's get started."

Standing at the counter, Duke announced eagerly. "Okay, I got the stuff."

Cat instructed Duke on how to mix the ingredients and cook them on the griddle. They made plain, banana and blueberry pancakes. While Cat cooked bacon, sausage, and ham steaks, Duke flipped pancakes. By 8:30, there were grits, home fries, hash browns and French toast warming in chafing dishes. There were scrambled eggs with cheese and some with peppers and onions along with toast, biscuits, and English muffins. The brothers arrived just as everything was ready to serve. Cat smiled at Duke. She glanced down and noticed fresh scratches on his arms

"What happened?" She asked concerned.

Confused Duke looked at her strangely. Didn't she remember last night when she fought him? "Cat, you don't remember?"

"Remember what?" She asked confusion on her face.

"You and I...,"

Cat put her fist to her hips; her eyes narrowed. "If you say we made mad passionate love Ellington, I swear I'm going to crown you with your own pots," she huffed and walked away.

Amazed Duke frowned after her. She honestly didn't remember.

Are you two at it again?" Zoey accused coming into the kitchen.

"Good Morning Pud; Mornin' Zo," they greeted together.

"How was your evening?" Cat asked as she pulled two pitchers of orange juice from the fridge.

"Great we had a good time," she answered noticing the food on the table. "I know Duke didn't....,"

Indignantly her brother answered. "No Zola, Caitlin lost a bet, your greedy brothers are now pulling into the driveway as we speak."

Zoey looked at all the food prepared. "Cat, you did this for those scavengers?"

"Yep, Ellington made the pancakes and..." Just then the brothers barreled in the house.

Walking between Dizzy and Satch was Yaz; with Cab and Jelly bringing up the rear, each man scowling, but Yaz was grinning.

"Morning Sassy," he greeted.

"Morning Yaz," she blushed smiling. "You're early."

Duke frowned at his brothers. "What's going on?"

"Tell me this Playa didn't spend the night Zola?" Cab growled.

"None ya," she replied taking Yaz's hand pulling him away from her deranged brothers. "Mind if we have breakfast here?" She asked Yaz ignoring her other brothers.

"No," Yaz replied allowing Zoey to lead him to the table where they sat and quietly begin to talk.

The brothers glared at Duke, and Cat glared at them and then at Duke. "Like I said morons," she commented and joined Yaz and Zoey.

"Come moron's let's eat," Duke invited leaving them.

When the brothers saw all the delicious food laid out, Yaz and Zoey were forgotten. After they had blessed the food, they dug into the food ravenously.

"Don't eat the pancakes, Duke made them," Zoey warned. Any of them that had pancakes on their plates placed them back into the dish. Duke and Cat laughed and placed one of each pancake on their plate and began eating.

"Ellington these are delicious, you did a good job," she complimented ignoring the faces his brothers and sister made.

Jelly reached over and took a cut of banana pancake on her plate popping it in his mouth. "Damn these are good," and went and got some of his own. Yaz did the same.

"They are good." He offered some to Zoey. Cautiously she tasted them.

"Duke did not make these," Zoey accused.

"Yes he did," Cat confirmed.

Cat stared at the now empty serving dishes. The six large men consumed every crumb except for a few pieces of toast and muffins.

"Thanks, Cat," they chorused grinning.

Cat stood to her feet. "Just so you know it was from the kindness of my heart that I was more than happy to prepare this breakfast for you because I know each one of you cheated last night," she stated calmly.

They had the nerve to feign surprise and declared they didn't cheat.

"So for your punishment you all will wash dishes and clean the kitchen," she stated with arms folded over her chest glaring at each one like disobedient little boys. Duke and Zoey laughed. Yaz folded his lip to keep from smiling. Grumbling they began to clear off the table.

"Come on Duke," Cab growled.

"Oh no, Ellington did not cheat last night," Cat intervened. "The sooner you start, the sooner you will be done."

Cat ignored the grumbling and complaining as she spoke to Zoey and Yaz about their evening. Duke listened closely. He had to agree Yaz Bryant was a decent man, and he appeared to genuinely care for Zoey. Maybe he could relax a little now where Zoey was concerned.

They heard a loud crash and clatter and then bickering coming from the kitchen.

"Don't make me come in there!" Cat called loudly.

Satch pushed open the swinging door. "Jelly was spinning a plate on his finger," Satch reported.

"Punk!" they all heard and laughed.

"We're going to Hershey Park," Zoey shared grinning.

"Hershey Park?" Cat inquired.

"It's an amusement park," Zoey explained simply. "Want to come?" She invited.

Cat shook her head. "No, this is a time for you and Yaz."

"Come on Cat, it will be fun," Yaz invited.

"Fun where?" Jelly asked as he joined the group.

"Yaz and Zoey are going to Hershey Park," she answered.

"Hershey!!" voices chorused behind them.

"We're going," Cab stated.

Duke shrugged. "Why not, we'll all go. Caitlin and I will ride with Yaz and Zoey; you four take my Hummer.

It turned out to be a lovely day, except for whenever Yaz looked as if he wanted to kiss Zoey, Cab, Satch, Dizzy and Jelly were there to stop him. Cat and Duke just shook their heads, but overall the day was good. Cat sat beside Duke looking down at the angry scratches on his arms

"You never told me what happened to your arm," Cat commented.

Duke frowned. "Cat you did this," He stated.

Cat countered. "I did not."

Duke frowned confused. "You really don't remember?"

Cat stared at him for a long moment before her eyes lowered. She was racking her brain to remember. She didn't see Duke as a liar. He was too stern and arrogant for that. She could not recall any of it. Her eyes shut tightly. Did I black out again? She asked herself. Other than the nightmares she didn't remember the next day and the one time when one of her male coworkers grabbed her from behind in the small Breakroom at her job; she snapped, and it took him fifteen minutes to calm her down. She was so distraught he had to help her get home. The next day at the office, he apologized, and she didn't know what he was talking about. As the day worn on flashes of what he claimed happened came to her. Later that night she went online to research the symptoms of waking blackouts and short-term memory loss. She discovered she was mentally defective due to some violence in the past she didn't remember unless something triggered it. She had dissociation disorder or repressed memory syndrome according to what she read. She thought about going to a doctor for help. When she read that antidepressants, tranquilizers, and anti-anxiety medication would be part of the treatment, along with hypnosis and different types of therapy she dropped that idea. She did not want to remember the past she didn't know she had. It was bad enough she had nightmares and she was well aware of her blackouts. Normally she was able to push them away when something triggered memories of her past; which she could remember vaguely. She did not want to face it, but the blackouts and the nightmares were now coming frequently and more severely. Cat rose and quickly walked away.

"Cat!" Duke called following after her. He caught her turning to face. Tears slipped down her face. "I would never hurt you, Ellington," her tone choked. "Not on purpose." She turned to leave. Duke grabbed her hand. "I know that Caitlin, tell me what's going on?" He asked concerned. Her eyes lowered to his arms, and she gently touched him. "I did do this didn't I?" Duke stared at her wanting to understand.

"I'm sorry--I so sorry," she groaned ashamed and quickly left Duke losing herself in the crowd of people ignoring Duke calling her name.

Duke didn't know how long he stood there dumbfounded when his phone vibrated by his side indicating a text message. "Cat's not well, taking her home, ride with your brothers, Zoey."

Duke quickly texted her back. "Don't leave yet. Where are you?"

"On PA Turnpike." Duke cursed.

He sighed. "Okay see you at home." Duke then texted Cab. "Let's go, I'm at the pavilion."

Chapter Nine

Yaz lay in bed with his arms folded behind his head staring blankly at the ceiling. The team arrived at the training camp a week ago, and right away they went into drills and practice plays, and he was exhausted. He had Dr. Zoey Howard to thank. At first, he experienced fear that his knee would not hold up and messed up a few plays. After being checked by the trainer, and team doctor who assured he was one hundred percent, he went back out on the field and played like he has never gotten injured.

He smiled when he thought about Zoey. A few days before camp he and Zoey shared breakfast, lunch, and dinner finding himself becoming much attached to the sassy woman. Even her brothers loosened up on him. They no longer gave him the third degree when he picked her up. Despite their threats of bodily harm, if he hurt her, he found he liked all the brothers. He liked the way they looked out each other and was not ashamed to say they loved one another and Zoey had them wrapped around her little finger. Oh, they tried to be tough with her, but she just broke them down. That's the kind of family he wanted. He knew he would never have that with the family he now had, especially after learning of their deceit. As far as he was concerned he had no family. Had he married Trish..., no he did not want to think about that either.

Yaz chuckled. He liked Zoey more that he thought himself capable of after the hurt he endured by Trish Devereaux's dainty little hands. After that experience, he vowed he would never let another woman get close enough to break his heart ever again, and that included Sassy. No matter how much he enjoyed being with her, he would not let himself fall for her.

72

He would be lying if he said he didn't want her in his bed. He wanted her, there was no doubt about that, but he did not want to start something he knew he could not finish. Zoey wanted him. He could smell her delicious arousal every time their kissing was out of control, and he knew without a doubt if he pressed her, he'd have her withering beneath, but he refrained. He didn't want to hurt Zoey when he got tired of her. He sensed her innocence. Zoey was the sort of woman a man married, not have occasional booty calls. All he could offer Zoey is friendship, despite the lust he felt whenever they were together. He decided, after Training Camp, he would tell her all he could offer was friendship, convince her it was better that way. He didn't want to be in love, and Zoey deserved a man who would love her unconditionally. When he finally fell asleep, he slept fitfully. Dreams of Zoey haunted him. One minute he was making wild passionate love to Zoey and the next Trish's beautiful passion filled face looked up at him.

Three months had passed, and Zoey knew soon Yaz would be home. As she lay in her bed, her thoughts were all on Yaz. She talked to him every night since he left. Zoey smiled, glowing in the love she felt for him. When he returned, she would allow the relationship to go further. The last time they spoke, he said they had a lot to discuss. She tried to get him to tell her over the phone, but he wanted to wait until they saw each other. Suddenly the nightly conversation stopped. When he first went to training camp, he called every night. Zoey scolded herself. He was occupied with training and maybe too exhausted to talk, which is understandable. Zoey closed her eyes and dreamt of the man she loves.

Totally exhausted after practice, Yaz threw his battered body across the bed. In a week, he would be home; pre-season would start, and he will have that needed talk with Zoey. His plan was to be honest as he could be without hurting her feelings. He knew she was feeling him just as he knew he was feeling her. It was not ready to open his heart. Zoey was understanding; all he had to do was be honest with her.

Tonight the coach gave them the weekend off, and the team was going into town to a club. They needed to relax and forget the aches and pains. He would kill for one of Zoey's massages. His phone vibrated on the nightstand. He looked at the screen, unavailable it read. Relieved it was not Zoey, he answered the phone.

"Yeah?"

"Yazy," a familiar voice spoke. A voice he would never forget or want to hear from again.

"Trish?" Yaz sounded surprised. She repeated his name softly. Instantly anger trapped his body in the past.

"How did you get my number?" He asked brusquely.

"I have been trying to get in touch with you for a long time. I found Jim's number, and he gave it to me. I hope...,"

Yaz interrupted her. What do you want Trish?" He inquired harshly. Silence.

"Goodbye, Trish."

"No! Yazy, please wait. I know you hate me. I don't blame you. I was cold and calculating, and I used you terribly," she replied southern drawl thick.

"Used Trish is quite mild, you broke my heart!" He nearly shouted into the phone.

"I'm sorry, please, believe me, I'm so sorry," she exclaimed desperation in her voice. "Please hear me out."

"Yaz I need help and you were the only person that came to mind. I know I hurt you and I have regretted it the past eight years. I know it was wrong, and I should have followed my heart and stayed with you. They would have disowned me if I stayed with you. I was selfish, and for that, I apologize. I am no longer that person," she confessed.

Yaz listened unsure if he believed she cared. "Fine Trish, what do you want? He asked harshly.

"How are you doing?"

"Trish I don't have time for this," he replied impatiently.

"Okay, Okay. I need to see you, can we meet someplace?" She asked.

"Trish I'm in training camp," he snapped.

"I know, Jim told me where I can find you. I arrived in Philadelphia early this morning and drove all the way to Allentown to see you. I wouldn't have contacted you if it was not necessary.

Yaz sighed loudly. What happened to them was in the past and he was over Trish. So why did it still hurt so much after all these years?

"Yaz?"

"Okay, Trish where are you?"

She gave him the hotel where she stayed. Trish was the only woman he ever loved other than his mom. Back then, she was everything to him. Hell, he was going to marry her. Yaz shook his head and prayed he wasn't making a mistake by seeing her again.

"Mornin' Duke," Zoey greeted cheerfully pouring coffee into her favorite mug.

"Mornin' Pud," he responded behind his morning paper. "Hungry?"

"No time. I have a few patients this morning, but I'll be free at noon."

"Oh, you and Yaz made plans since he has returned?" Duke asked still buried behind the paper.

Zoey frowned. Yaz has returned. He never told her when he was coming home, but then he stopped calling her every night. She even tried to call him, but his voice mail picked up. An unexplainable tightness formed in her chest. Duke moved the paper looking at her a frowning Zoey.

"Pud are you all right?"

"Oh yeah," she answered absently. "I'm fine just a lot on my mind. I have to go." Zoey kissed his cheek and left.

Zoey pulled into Yaz's driveway and parked beside his car. If he is back, why didn't he call me? She wondered. She got out of her car going to the door and rang the doorbell.

The door opened, and Miss Lilly stood a scowl on her round face.

"Mornin' Miss Lilly," Zoey greeted smiling.

"Hello, Zoey what are you doing here?" She asked sternly.

Zoey frowned. Something was wrong.

"Is Yaz back?"

Miss Lilly eyes shifted as she nodded.

"Can I see him?" Zoey asked.

"Come back...,"

"Miss Lilly, Trish wants breakfast in bed, could you..., Zoey," Yaz replied stunned to see her.

Miss Lilly looked at Yaz with disgust in her eyes. "Look Yazair, I'm not a maid, I'm a housekeeper. You want a maid you need to hire one," she snapped and stormed off.

Still standing in the doorway, Zoey asked. "What's going on Yaz?"

"How are you Zoey?"

"Can I come in?" She asked. Yaz moved so she could enter. They stood in the foyer, and the tension in the small area was thick. Something was not right and Yaz has yet to meet her eyes, for more than a second.

"How are you Zoey?" He repeated.

"How long have you been back? She countered.

"A week," he answered still not looking at her.

"Why didn't...?" She started to ask, but she knew why now. "Just tell me Yaz?" She insisted.

"Yaz!" a high-pitched female voice called.

Zoey eyes shifted to the sound of the voice and then back him.

"Zoey let me explain...,"

"Explain?" Zoey interrupted. "You have nothing to explain to me."

"I feel like..." He paused.

Zoey shook her head. "Why? You act as if we were lovers or something. We had fun together and I knew we were just friends," she exclaimed.

Just as, Yaz was about to speak, a beautiful fair skinned woman come into the foyer barefoot and wearing one of Yaz's practice jerseys that fell mid-thigh on her. She ignored Zoey.

"Yaz you need to take your servants in hand. The maid refuses to bring my breakfast...," The woman paused and rudely-eyed Zoey from her feet to the top of her head.

"Who is she?" She asked in a demanding tone.

Zoey glanced at Yaz, who squirmed with guilt.

"Hi, I'm Dr. Zoey Howard, Mr. Bryant's sports doctor, and Physical Therapist. I came to see how he made out in camp," Zoey explained.

"Oh," the woman sneered. "Don't be long Yazy," she replied leaving them alone.

Yaz knew Zoey didn't expect this. The expression on her face as she stared at him was burning a hole in his chest. She was right; they never made a commitment; they were free to see others.

"That's it!" Miss Lilly yelled.

Without another word, Zoey turned and left so he could deal with his domestic problems.

"I have had it with your Princess Yaz, I quit! She stormed.

"Miss Lilly please, I'll talk to her...,"

"You said that before," she interrupted. Yaz dropped his head.

Miss Lilly glared at him her hands firmly on her wide hips. What did you do to Zoey?"

"What do you mean?" He frowned.

"You don't know what you want, do you, boy?" Miss Lilly chastised. "You just broke the heart of the best thing in your dysfunctional life," she said pushing him out of her way. "Oh, and Henri quit yesterday," she called over her shoulder. Yaz dropped his head, cursed slamming the door shut.

What was wrong with him? Trish has only been in back in his life for one week, and all hell has broken loose, and he knew it had only just begun. In his heart, he knew he was breaking Zoey's heart, he could see it on her face although she tried to cover it up. Wait until Zoey's brother finds out he broke her heart.

Zoey will understand that Trish was his first love. Although, he had not seen her since the night of their college graduation, it surprised him that there was still that dim spark. When he met her that night in Allentown, he knew how he fell in love with her. Even after all these years, she was more beautiful than he remembered, more mature and sexier. When she opened the door and saw him, she fell into his arms and sobbed heart-wrenching tears. She told him how her ex-husband abused her. She wanted a divorce, but he refused, she explained, until she threatened to expose Congressman Beauford as a wife beater. He then conceded and gave her the divorce with no alimony or place to live. She couldn't go back to her parents they would make her go back to him just to avoid scandal.

This was a side of Trish he never saw, and it broke his heart. He hated to see her so distraught. He held her in his arms until she could control herself. The next thing he knew they were kissing and Trish was more skilled than he remembered. Before things got carried away, he put a stop to her seduction. He was not ready to be right back where he left off, in love with Trish Devereaux-Beauford. This time, he did not have on rose colored glasses and moving cautiously with Trish was his only option, hence, the reason for the separate bedroom which Trish did not like. Now he had no housekeeper or chef. Yaz rubbed his hand vigorously over his close-cropped hair and went to talk to Trish again.

Yaz sat on the side of the bed feeling guilty for the way Zoey found out about Trish. Hell, didn't he just decide to be strictly friends with her because he was so afraid of getting hurt again by a woman. But here he was back with the same woman that stomped on his heart, causing him to hurt the one woman who brought him back to life, the woman only that genuinely cared about him.

"Damn," he muttered. The pain on her face was killing him, and he needed to explain things to her as soon as possible. It is not your fault; she shouldn't have come here; an evil voice echoed in his head.

"No, she had every right to come," he said softly. He had to talk to Zoey.

Yaz could hear Trish, the beautiful heartbreaker, splashing in the tub. Even after all these years, she still had a hold on him. He recalled the conversation they had when he asked her if her parents knew she was with him. Instantly the tear came as she spoke.

"Yaz the biggest mistake I ever made was not telling my parents I wanted you. But what could I do? They are my parents and name and prestige are all they know. It was a mistake to marry Beauford; he was cruel and mean to me. You have to believe I only married him to please my parents."

"What about now? How do you think your parents are going to feel when they find out you are with your black pet?" He asked harshly remembering the words he would never forget.

"Oh Yaz," she cried. "I did not mean that. It was just to stop Momma from prying," she explained and started to sob incoherently, begging him to forgive her. All he could do was hold her until her tears subsided. "I just want to be happy again, I want you Yaz only you."

Yaz stared at the closed bathroom door. Was he making another mistake with Trish? He did not hesitate to tell her that he wore the pants, and she would not be wrapping him around her fingers this time. Years ago, he accepted her spoiled and pampered ways, but now he saw her as the vain, selfish person she truly is. He would treat her well, but he would not be catering to her every whim.

Trish Devereaux-Beauford was no one's fool. She knew that there was more to Yaz and that doctor. "Well little doctor, Yaz is mine," she muttered. When Jim called her, it was a godsend. Her parents were broke and Beauford divorced her giving her nothing. It was stupid to sign that prenuptial, but her mother insisted she sign it telling her once she had Beauford wrapped she could suggest he tear it up. She would have probably gotten at least a million if she didn't forget the clause about adultery, causing her to forfeit any support from him. She could not go back to her parent's home; they damn near sold everything they owned only living off the money from the almost defunct grocery store chain or what were left of them. Jim's calling gave her hope, and as long as she gets what she wants, she didn't mind helping Jim. He told her all she had to do was break up the little fling with the doctor and convince Yaz to take him back. This was too easy she thought smugly. She was sure she could wrap Yaz around her finger if only he would share his bed with her. When he informed her, they would not be sharing a bed she protested, and when she couldn't get him to bend on this, she gave up for the moment. Yaz would come around eventually she was sure of that. He had loved her once, and she will have him loving her again.

Trish lay back in the tub sighing contently. Yes, this was too easy. Once she got Yaz believing she has changed and loved him deeply, she would marry him and this time, there would be no prenup. The first thing she needed to do was some shopping, since all her clothes were at her parents packed in boxes, and she was not going back to be lectured about how her scandalous behavior ruined the Devereaux's good name. Yaz will take care of and give her all she desires. With a contented smile on her face, her eyes closed.

Zoey canceled all her appointments. She was in no condition to see anyone right now and needed some time to overcome this obstacle and get herself together. With Duke out of town and her brothers still at work, she would not have to answer any unwanted questions.

She lay in a fetal position in her darkened bedroom, the acute pain she felt was nothing she has ever experienced before. Tears seeped from her tightly closed eyes. She had to get over this, Yaz never said they were a couple. True, they just went out every day and spoke on the phone a few times a day, but that didn't mean they were a couple. He was her friend. Then why did his kisses make her think he was like a man drowning? Only stopping just before things got out of control, no matter how she prayed that he didn't stop making her feel so good.

Her cell kept ringing, and she would look at the screen. It was Yaz, and she simply ignored it, deleting his messages without listening to them. She was not ready to face Yaz or anyone, especially her brothers. They had warned her against seeing pro athletes, but she thought Yaz was different, he was different. She knew how some pro athletes went through women, she had five brothers, but Yaz was not like that. She groaned when a sharp pain went through her making her clucked her chest and curling into a tighter ball, and she sobbed until she fell into a fitful sleep.

Zoey woke to the sound of Duke's voice coming through the intercom, and she placed a pillow over her head, not ready to face anyone.

"Okay Pud, I guess you're out," she heard him say.

Tomorrow she would see Duke she promised herself, she couldn't lay here and wallow in misery, she had patients who needed her. She didn't have that luxury of indulging in depression, plus she is made of sterner stuff and she will get over this. All she needed was a long hot soak in her luxurious marble bathtub, and then she needed to tell Duke about her and Yaz. She's never kept secrets from her older brother, and after she tells him what has happened, she will demand his promise, and the promise of her brothers not to retaliate against Yaz.

Feeling better, Zoey went in search of Duke. She found him in his enormous study bent over some papers.

She stood in the doorway. "Duke," she called softly.

"Hi Pud, give me a minute," he said still bent over his papers. "Okay." His head lifted. Duke frowned when he saw the unhappy, puffy eyes of his baby sister.

"Zola, what's wrong baby?" He shouted coming from behind the massive mahogany desk to stand before her, his eyes concerned.

Tears welled in her eyes. "Duke, I...," she could get the words out.

Duke pulled her into his arms while she sobbed against his chest. "Come on Baby sit down, tell me what's wrong." Zoey let Duke lead her to the large leather sofa. "You okay?" He asked gently handing her his handkerchief.

She nodded while she blew her nose and wiped her eyes.

"Tell me Pud, what's going on?"

Zoey told him everything. She told him how she and Yaz talked every night while he was away and when the calls stopped. She told him about the half-dressed woman at his house when she went to see him. When she finished talking Duke rose from beside her. The scowl on his face was not a healthy sign.

"I warned him!" He roared.

"No Duke, please. It is not his fault. He never said we were a couple, and just because I fell in love with him doesn't mean he had to fall for me," she stated.

"Yeah baby, but he led you to believe that it could be something. I saw you together, and I could have sworn he had feelings for you."

"No Duke, he didn't lead me on," she shrugged. "I just read more into it than there was. All I ask is that you and our brothers do nothing to him," she paused looking into his eyes.

Duke grunted and turned away. Zoey moved behind him and slipped her arms around his waist, pressing her face to his back. "You have to promise me, please. I already feel crappy."

"Pud you are asking a lot," he grumbled.

Zoey stepped back. "Duke, please. Tell them not to bother Yaz. This is not his fault, he promised me nothing," she implored.

Duke turned to face her. "How can you ask this of me Zoey when I can see he hurt you?"

"Duke please; he is your client now, let it go. I'm embarrassed enough."

"Pud I don't know if I can keep these promises," Duke stated.

"If you and our brothers do anything to him, I swear I will leave here and never come back. I mean it Ellington!' she shouted, quickly leaving a stunned Duke.

"Damn it!" Duke shouted as he headed to the fitness room to pretend his body bag was Yaz Bryant.

It had been two weeks since Yaz has seen or heard from Zoey since she was ignoring his calls. All he wanted is to explain to her about Trish. He just wanted to say he knew he hurt her, beg for forgiveness, and that it was not his intention. Duke called him to discuss plans for the season, and he was dreading the meeting. He was sure the brothers knew about him and Zoey by now.

Yaz stepped off the elevator to the Howard Consultant floor.

"Hello Mr. Bryant," the receptionist greet, "the brothers are waiting in the conference room."

I just bet they are, probably with plastic spread out on the floor. "Thank you," Yaz replied.

Yaz entered the large room. Duke, Cab, Dizzy, and Satch rose from their seats. "Come on in Yaz, have a seat," Duke invited. Yaz sat and the brothers followed suit.

Duke cleared his throat. "Before we get started, let's get something straight. Business is business, anything that happens outside this building has no business here."

Satch glared at Yaz. "Thank Zoey for my not kicking your ass."

"That's enough Satch," Duke ordered.

"I never meant to hurt Zoey, I--I." Duke raised his hand in mid-sentence.

"It's over, let it be," he said through clenched teeth.

Yaz nodded his agreement, as did the others. During the meeting, Yaz was amazed at the plans they had for him, and everything they proposed was for his best interest. His contract was pending with the Stallions, and he truly wanted to stay in Philly. Duke he knew would negotiate his contract and get him the best deal available, and if he continued to do as well as he is, he knew Duke would get him top dollar, and a longer contract. However, there were other teams interested in him, but his heart is set on staying in Philly. At the conclusion of the meeting, each brother shook his hand, a little firmer than other times, and Duke walked him out.

Duke, I'm sorry, I never meant to hurt Zoey," he sighed not knowing what else to say.

"For some reason, I believe you. I think you are an honorable man Yaz, and Zoey will be alright, just stay away from her, so she can heal. That is all I ask."

There it was. Could he stay away? Could he not talk to her ever again? He realized at that moment that he would deeply miss Zoey, yet he had to do as Duke asked, if only to give Zoey time to heal.

Zoey threw herself into her practice, not bothering to take time for herself. She doubled her patient roster and occupational therapy appointments. Although she told her brothers she was fine, her actions did not reflect that. She needed someone to talk to, but Cat was away on business, and her brothers were over every night smothering her. All she knew was as long as she was busy, she didn't have time to think about Yaz. Tomorrow night will be David's annual anniversary franchise party and all involved with the team was encouraged to attend. Players, coaches, managers, and trainers; even the cheerleaders were invited. She had always attended his parties only because David pressured her into it. This year she was not attending no matter how hard David pressured her. Her brothers all thought it would be good for her to go however during dinner, she informed her brothers she was not going. She later admitted to Duke she was not attending this year for fear of running into Yaz.

"Pud, you can't hide. You are going to see him sooner or later." Zoey stubbornly shook her head.

"Listen," he said. "What is it that women do to show a man she is over him?"

Zoey sucked her teeth. "How should I know Duke? I've never dated before and been dumped."

"You have not been dumped Pud," he consoled.

"What do you call it?" She grated out.

"That's not the point. Go to David's party, put on your best dress, not pants or what you usually wear, put on something like you wore that night Yaz took you to dinner, but not that dress," Duke added with a smile.

Zoey frowned rolling her eyes. "Oh, I see, you want me to make Yaz jealous," she replied unbelieving her older brother was inciting her to play games.

Duke shook his head. "No, I want him to see what he passed up."

"Same thing Duke," she muttered. Anyway, how can I make him jealous when he was not interested in the first place?" She shouted pushing from the table rising.

"Trust me Pud, he was interested," he assured her.

"I don't like games Duke. He's with who he wants and I'm not going to the party!" She announced storming from the room.

Duke shook his head remorsefully. He hated seeing Zoey like this. She has not laughed in weeks and all she does is work non-stop. The brothers offered her a cruise, and she turned them down, saying she didn't have time for a cruise. He was at a loss and didn't know how to bring her out of this funk she was in.

"I'm going to punch Yaz in the face, maybe I will feel better," he muttered.

Chapter Ten

The night of the anniversary party, her brothers were dressed to the nines looking devilishly handsome, each coming by to give her one last argument and still she stubbornly she declined. Finally, they gave up and left her alone. Zoey sat in the den, order movies from Comcast, popped popcorn and sat with her legs curled under her. Didn't they understand, it was enough every Sunday she heard Yaz Bryant this and Yaz Bryant that. Or did you see how Yaz ran rings around the opposing team? Or how many touchdowns he made. She did not need to see him too.

The only thing she agreed with Duke about was she needed to show him that she was over him. Zoey groaned. When did she become such a coward? Her brothers taught her to face opposition head on, and that was exactly what she was going to do. She was nobody's punk.

Zoey went to her apartment and looked through all the clothes she brought when she and Cat went shopping, and there had to be something she could wear. Zoey pulled out one dress after the other tossing them on the bed.

"Yes," she breathed grinning. The Elle Saab evening gown was perfect.

"My hair," she groaned. Zoey lifted her hair to the top of her head. "That's it," she muttered. Matching the gown with her Jimmy Choo four inch navy crystal embellished sandals was perfect. She had time to pamper herself because the party didn't actually start until after dinner when all the mundane speeches were made, so she had time.

She slipped on the midnight blue evening gown that bared one shoulder while the other arm was covered in a long sleeve. The gown had pleated panels to the floor that highlighted the center slit to her upper thigh that expose a full leg when she walked. "Yes, this is the dress," she grinned. She was pleased with her elegant and sophisticated look, also with her hair up in loose curls and her subtle makeup enhanced her pretty face. She finished her look with her mother diamond stud earrings that twinkled when the light reflected off them, which set the dress off well. She looked beautiful.

Just after 9 pm, Zoey strolled into the Hyatt ballroom. She stood at the entrance admiring the invited guest all were dressed to impressed, and the team's players looked extremely handsome in their tuxes. She removed the silk stole she draped around her shoulders and checked it at the coat check. Slowly she strolled into the crowded room and could feel the eyes in the room following her as she made her way through smiling and greeting those she was already acquainted. Her smile widened when she realized they did not know who she was. Ahead she saw Duke in deep conversation with David, the Stallions owner, and best friend. She approached them and stood beside Duke slipping her hand under his elbow.

Duke looked down. "Pud?" He said as he studied her. Zoey grinned.

I'm a Howard, not a coward," she stated proudly.

"Little Bit," David said with a frown. "Is that you?"

"Yes," she blushed.

"You're beautiful," he swooned.

"Back off David," Duke warned.

"Where are my brothers over by the food I bet," Zoey inquired ignoring Duke.

Duke smiled presenting his elbow. "See ya later David."

Duke bent to whisper in her ear. "You think that dress is a little revealing?" Duke asked.

Don't start Duke," Zoey whispered back smiling.

On the search for the brothers, Zoey and Duke were stopped several times asking for an introduction to people she already knew. Duke laughed when he reintroduced his little sister to the people she already knew.

"There they are? She said when she approached her brothers.

"Satch put down that plate!" She ordered good-naturedly behind him.

Satch turned. "Little Bit?" he said as his eyes took in her appearance. "You look beautiful," he said grinning. "But I think...,"

"Don't start," she interrupted. She was now surrounded by her five brothers, each talking all at once voicing their concerns.

"Stop it, I'm fine," she told them smiling. "I want to have an enjoyable time that is all."

David broke into the group taking her hand. "This is my dance, Little Bit," he said pulling her from her stunned brothers. On the dance floor, David pulled her into his arms to do the Bop. David was the best Bopper she knew because he taught her everything she knew about bopping. "You game?" He challenged grinning. Zoey laughed. "Are you challenging me old man," she teased.

David turned and spun Zoey, and she was right in step with him. The other dancer cleared the floor and watched as the host and Zoey burned up the dance floor.

Zoey was having a marvelous time until she saw Yaz and his companion. It has been a while since she last saw him, and she did not want to relive the pain she gradually getting over. When she decided to come, she thought she could handle seeing him again, however now she wasn't so sure. Her heart began pattering against her chest and her stomach felt all fluttery. She was standing next to Byron Harris, one of the Stallions wide receivers. Right away she noticed, Yaz did not appear to be too happy, and his date's mouth was moving a mile a minute.

Although she saw her at Yaz's house a few weeks ago, Zoey still didn't know who she was. "Who's that with Yaz?" she asked Byron nonchalantly sipping her drink.

"Who? His pain in the ass," Byron commented.

"Really?" Zoey replied interested.

"Yeah, she calls Yaz 24/7. We were playing cards over his place one night, and she whined the whole time until we couldn't take her voice anymore and left. Oh damn, he's bringing her over," Byron groaned.

"See you later," Zoey said moving away.

"Oh no you don't Zo you have to see this first hand."

Her heart started to pound in her chest. She wasn't ready to talk to Yaz. Zoey took a deep, shaky breath. You can do this Zo, she coached herself, putting a smile on her face and slipping her hand under Byron's elbow.

The couple stopped in front of them.

"Hi, Sas…Zoey. What's up Bry?' Yaz greeted. "Dr. Zoey Howard this is Trish Devereaux."

Zoey smiled at her. "I saw her at your house a few weeks ago, didn't I?" Zoey asked.

"Yes, but you didn't know my name, Yaz and I are together again," she was saying a heavy southern drawl.

"Really were you apart?" Zoey asked.

"Yes, after college we were separated but now…,"

"Come on Zoey let's dance," Byron interrupted.

"Excuse us," Zoey called over her shoulder as Byron pulled her away.

"That was rude Bry," Zoey chastised now away from the loving couple. "But I'm glad you did it," she grinned.

Yaz watched as Byron pulled Zoey away and into his arms for a slow dance.

"Yaz get me a drink," Trish whined. Yaz was glad to do it, he would do anything to get a moment away from Trish.

Trish's eyes narrowed on Zoey as she danced. Jim was right. There was something going between Yaz and the doctor, and she would make it, her business to see the doctor and let her know Yaz was not available any longer.

Not long, Trish got her chance when she saw Zoey go into the ladies room. The bathroom was oddly empty. Zoey peered into the mirror freshening her lipstick when the door open, and another lady entered. Zoey glanced at Yaz's date when she entered the restroom and stood next to Zoey while putting on her lipstick.

"How close were you and Yaz? She asked blunted.

"Excuse me?"

"Yaz and you," she repeated in her southern accent.

"You need to ask Yaz," Zoey replied coolly. Zoey didn't like answering to anyone about her practice or her patients, and she was slowly getting pissed off.

"I'm asking you!" She snapped. "Because it appeared like there was more to me."

Zoey faced her. "I do not discuss my relationship with my patients, if you have any questions, you need to speak Yaz," Zoey stated calmly.

"Look, Honey," Trish said her eyes scanning Zoey distastefully. "Yaz is not available, we have a history we were college…."

"Yeah… Yeah, I know sweethearts, how romantic," Zoey replied sarcastically.

"That's right. Yaz loves me, always has, always will," her tone shrilled loudly.

"And your point is?" Zoey asked bored.

"Stay away from him. I will have him replace you as his doctor, and he will do it," she boasted.

"Look, I don't want Yaz, never did," she lied. "And if you have to warn me away, it seems you are not sure you have him yourself." Zoey moved to the door paused and looked back at Trish. "Ya'll have a good time, ya hear," Zoey said as he left the frustrated southern belle with her mouth gaped open.

Yaz and Trish drove in relative silence on the way home, each in deep thoughts. Yaz couldn't stop thinking about how beautiful Zoey looked and throughout the evening, he found himself searching for her. Every time he spotted her, at least, two or three men monopolizing and surrounding her, and it pissed him off. Where were her brothers? He had not expected to see Zoey and was surprised by her appearance, and couldn't stress how stunning she looked. He didn't like the attention she was attracting, as he watched her laughing and flirting with one of her admirers. His entire body tensed. He knew it shouldn't have bothered him that she was talking to other men, but it did.

Yaz glanced at Trish sulking beside him and shook his head. He made a mistake moving Trish into his home. Not only has he lost the best housekeeper and chef, but he also had to put up with Trish spoiled whiny ways. However, he did know that about her when they were together in college, but back then, he thought it was cute, now it got on his nerves. He would have given her carte blanche, but Cab advised him to put a limit on her spending, which he did. When he informed Trish of her limit, she turned a shade of red he had never seen on black women despite the fairness of the skin. This was a first. The Trish he remembered was always sweet and biddable. This Trish exploded. "All I'm worth to you is a measly twenty-five thousand dollars, Yaz," she shrieked. "I thought you loved me and would give me anything I desired," she whined. Yaz was too tired from practice to debate the issue. He simply told her, "I'm not changing it, Trish, it is more than enough." He walked away. This was the woman he loved at one time and wanted to give her the world. What happened? She was a mistake he was not going to entertain anymore.

Trish glanced at Yaz and rolled her eyes. He was not the same man she had wrapped around her finger in college. There was a time she had him whipped and if she asked him to rob a bank she was so sure he would have done it. Since she moved into his house, they had not been intimate once, and no amount of seduction she would throw at him changed that, and she came to the realization that he just didn't want her. She could feel her meal ticket slipping through her elegant fingers. Now she had to deal with Jim, who was on her back wanting to know if she persuaded Yaz to take him back yet. She tried but whenever she brought up the subject of Jim, Yaz refuses to talk about it. Also, she was lonely and she hated this dreary town, and Yaz did not care. He had taken her to a few of his teammates get-togethers so that she could meet some of the wives and girlfriends. Right away she knew she was going to like any of them. Then on top of that, those gutter rats had the nerve to ask her to volunteer with them at a fundraising yard sale to fund the after-school programs in the area public schools. Please, she could not be so bothered. They even asked her if she could donate any old clothes she didn't wear for the woman's shelter. She would burn them before she gave them to some poor women. Her blouses cost more than a full ensemble that they would wear. Soon the invitations stop coming, and that was fine with her. It didn't bother her, he never had females around her unless they were catering to her. Women tend to become jealous of her anyway. She looked over at Yaz and then turned to look out the window. Yaz was not making her feel special and she was not happy. He had the nerve to give her limit on her spending. At least with Beauford she had carte blanche. Now, Beauford, there's a man she had wrapped until he caught her in bed with his law partner, and now she had to get Yaz where she wanted him because she didn't do "poor" well.

Yaz opened the door for Trish and together they entered the house.

"You coming up Baby," Trish purred.

"In a little while," he muttered turning away. Trish sucked her teeth and stomped off.

Yaz went to his study unloosening his tie snatching it from around his neck and tossing it on the leather sofa. He went to the bar and poured himself a cognac then downing it in one swallow and refilling the snifter. He flopped down on the chair, extended long leg crossing them at the ankle, and stared at the amber liquor. He wondered if Zoey was still at the party. He wanted to stay hoping for a chance to dance with her, but Trish whined and pouted that she was ready to leave. He figured they might as well leave because Trish complained The whole time they were there. If it was not the food, it was the music, or commenting the northerner did not know how to give a classy party. When he asked her to dance, she refused to say, "Who does the jitterbug in an evening gown?" Saying she was not about to go out there, and get sweaty like those other women. So he sat quietly and watched as Zoey was again on the dance floor Boppin' with yet another man. Yaz heard the unmistakable sounds of the slow, hypnotic and smooth reggae tune with its exotic flair fill the room, and he could not help recalling the night Zoey danced with him. Yaz eyes narrowed when she began to sway her hips while sandwiched between two of his teammates, in his opinion too close. It was distressing enough that the slit of her gown opened to her upper thigh and she now had her gown lifted exposing her shapely legs as she pumped and gyrated her hips provocatively. One of the men dancing grabbed her by the waist pulling her against him and Zoey didn't stop the man she continued circling and wringing her behind against him. He had enough. Pushing his chair from the table and without a word to Trish, Yaz got up with the intent to snatch her off that damn dance floor. Weaving his way through the clusters of guests Yaz heading straight to the dance floor, only to be blocked by Zoey's five brothers that were now glaring at him.

"Don't even think about it Yaz," Duke warned.

Anger was in the eyes still glued on Zoey, Yaz growled at the formidable Howard clan. "You're just going to let that pervert rub up against her?

"Let it be," Jelly advised. "I still want to kick your ass for hurting Zo, but we promised her we would not hurt you.

"That's right Yaz, you made your choice," Satch commented nonchalantly. "Bad choice, but you made it.

"Maybe we should add a psychiatrist to the staff for those clients that don't know their ass from a hole in the wall," Dizzy commented to his brothers.

Cab placed a heavy hand on his shoulder shaking his head sadly. "Let it go Yaz."

Chapter 11

Yaz took a sip from the glass and focused on the present. Now alone, he realized the Howard's were right. He did choose and inadvertently hurting and losing his calm. He rubbed his hand roughly down his face, exhaled and tossing back remaining liquor then glanced at his Rado Swiss watch. It was already a couple of hours passed midnight and Zoey should be home now. He needed to talk to her and needed to know if she were all right. At least, that would be his excuse for going to her house so late. He punched in her number and waited for her to answer. "Damn," he muttered when the voice mail picked up. Yaz tensed when an absurd thought ran through his head. Did one of her many admirers seduce her into leaving with them? His heart slammed in his chest at the thought of some man making love to Zoey. He cursed, more confused than ever. Zoey was making him feel things he never felt before. He has never been a jealous man before Zoey, so why was he feeling an emotion he had no right feeling. Was the bastard now holding her as he long to do, kissing and tasting her sweetness? "Hell no!" He shouted coming to his feet.

Yaz didn't think twice and was out the door sitting behind the wheel of his Corvette speeding out of his driveway and didn't slow down until he was sitting in the private driveway of Zoey's apartment. He was on a mission, and not even Duke was going to stop him. He would not rest until he knew for sure she was alone. Her car was parked in the driveway, and a light was on in the living room, but that didn't mean she was alone. "To hell with this," he muttered and he got out of the car.

Zoey sat with her legs curled under her. She should be tired, but she was oddly invigorated. She danced until her feet were screaming to be released. A mischievous smile curled her lips when she recalled Yaz approaching her brothers with his southern belle. She was talking to Duke when the couple approached.

"Goodnight Duke," Yaz said shaking his hand.

"Leaving so soon?" Duke inquired. Yaz nodded and cut his eyes to Trish as she glared at Zoey.

"Well, Goodnight Yaz. Goodnight Tasha," Zoey said as friendly as she was able. She still couldn't believe that heifer had the nerve to warn her away from Yaz.

"It's Trisha," she said through clenched teeth.

Zoey shrugged. "Oops..., Sorry. Goodnight then." She moved away from the group. She could feel Trish eyes boring a hole in her back. The brothers only shook their heads and Yaz had to fold his lips to keep from smiling, but Zoey noticed before she turned to leave the couple. She shook her head thinking how incredible he looked and how miserable he is, also noticing he did not dance one time. Pity he is such a great dancer.

Zoey exhaled. Tired of thinking about Yaz, she begins to read her latest romance novel to begin living her life vicariously through the fictional characters. Thank goodness, she had no appointments tomorrow, because she had a feeling she would be up all night as she lost herself in the novel.

Just as she was about to get to the crucial plot of the book, a knock sounded on her door. Frowning, who would be at her door at three in the morning? It could not be Duke, he saw Duke leaving with Vicky and knew he was not coming home tonight. Her other brothers also had their dalliances too. So, who could be crazy enough to come here at this hour?

"Yes!" She called through the door.

"Zola, its Yaz, open up!" He ordered rather harshly.

Zoey snatched open the door. "What are doing here?" She asked indecorously. "Shouldn't you be home with your southern belle?"

Yaz pushed passed her looking around her living room. Zoey frowned at his back.

"What are you looking for?"

"You're alone!" He replied surprised.

"Why wouldn't I? Exasperated Zoey shook her head and repeated her previous question. "What are you doing here?

Yaz took in her appearance. All she had on was an old football jersey and nothing else he suspected. Damn she was sexy with her hair pinned loosely on top of her head.

"Yaz what do you want? Zoey asked again.

"I miss you." the admission came surprisingly easy for him.

"Too bad, get out," she countered moving toward the door. Yaz reached out as she passed pulling her to him so swiftly she crashed into his hard body, his arms quickly closing around her holding her.

Zoey tried to pull away. "Let me go, and you go home to your woman. And, by the way, if she threatens me away from you again, I'm going to dot her eye!" She threatened.

Yaz let her go. "Trish warned you to stay away from me?" Yaz asked now angry.

"Yep and you need to pull in your pet. I'm not the only one who finds her disagreeable. The player's wives tried to include her in some of their charity events. She told them that she did not do charities, let alone work. Your choice in women needs some work Yaz. First Memo Paris and now Scarlett O'Hara." she shook her head tsking.

Yaz sighed. Trish lied again. She told him the wives ignored her when she tried to get to know them.

Zoey stared at his dismal yet annoyed expression. "Yaz why are you here? She tried again.

He shook his head. "I don't know Sassy; I don't know what I'm doing anymore. Can I tell you about Trish, maybe you can help me understand what I'm doing?"

"Why...?

"Please, Sassy I need your calm," he implored.

"Zoey exhaled. "Come on in then," she invited reluctantly. "Can I get you something to drink?"

"No I just need to talk," he said sitting on the sofa, Zoey sat beside him putting distance between them.

A minute had passed before Yaz spoke. "Sassy, I'm sorry about hurting you, It--it was not my intention."

"I know that Yaz. It's not like we were a couple. We just hung out a few times."

Yaz chuckled. "Try every day."

"Okay every day," she admitted dourly. "We were friends."

"Yeah, even I knew there was something building between us. I felt it every time we kissed."

Zoey groaned. "Please, Yaz I don't want to hear this."

"It's the truth, and you know it. I ruined it for us when I...,"

"Tell me about you and Trish," she interrupted.

Yaz told her how head over heels in love he was with Trish while attending college wanting to give her the world. So much so, that while attending classes and playing football, he worked two jobs so he could give her all she wanted. His grade started to slip and was almost kicked off the team. What saved his ass was his talent, so the coaches gave him a chance.

Zoey sat quietly listening as he told his story. "I told her, I was not able to do it anymore. That should have been my first red flag. She didn't speak to me for weeks."

"What made her start, some pretty bauble, or something," Zoey asked sardonically.

Yaz looked directly in Zoey's eyes. "Yes," he answered. "I realize now, even then I was in love with her outer beauty. Then, I began making excuses to my teammates and friends for the ugliness inside her."

"So why do you feel compelled to share this with me Yaz? Why...," she paused when Yaz took her hand and began gently caressing it. Zoey tried to pull away, but he held it firmly.

"Because I need to understand why and I need the calm you bring out in me Sassy. I don't know why or how you do it, I just know you do."

Zoey heart melted at his words. This was a mistake letting him inside her home. She was over her infatuation. So why did her heart beat against her chest and her stomach seemed to be in knots?

Yaz let her hand go, and continued to tell her about his relationship with Trish. "I arrived late at the graduation party her parents had given her. When I found her, she was with her mother. I overheard her mother telling her, I was too dark to be a part of their family."

"What?"

"Yes. However, the words that stung the most was when her mother asked if she loves me. Her words were, and I quote, "I was not made to be a football player's wife, I'm first lady stock." Yaz paused. "I thought I loved her, or at least what I thought love was about." Yaz stood moving to the marble mantle.

"So why are you with her now Yaz if she said all those hurtful things?"

"I don't know. When she showed up in Allentown, crying and saying she needed to see me, which I at first refused. The more she cried...," he shook head disgustedly.

"How did she know where you were," Zoey interrupted with her question, knowing family and friends are not allowed during the first weeks of training.

"She called Jim," he stated. "I met her at the hotel she checked into. She is divorced now and told me her congressman husband abused her. In order for her to get her divorce, she threatened to expose him to the press as a wife beater. She left everything, relinquishing alimony and property. She has nothing so I guess I felt sorry for her.

"She couldn't go to her parents?"

"Her parents are about social standing, her divorcing a wealthy African-American congressman was scandalous, and she claimed they refused to help her.

Zoey listened to his tale of woe. Something just did not jell with her story. No judge or lawyer for that matter would have allowed the husband not to pay anything unless he had a cause, or she refused compensation. She could have gotten all she wanted just to keep quiet, and Trish didn't seem like a woman would give up possibly millions.

"I've heard your story Yaz, and I still have to ask, why are you here?"

"I need you to understand...,"

She hated to ask, but she needed to know how he felt about her. "Do you still love her after all this time?"

"When I first saw her and listened as she told me what happened, yes I thought something was still there," he admitted honestly.

"And now?"

"I see her for what she is. I realized I never really love her at all. I now see Trish for the selfish person she is, and I haven't slept with her if you are wondering."

Zoey jumped from the sofa. "And why would I care? I don't want to hear this," she said covering her ears.

"I'm sorry Zoey. Talk to me, I don't know what to do."

"If you are not happy, get rid of her, or find out if what she says is true. Your southern belle does not strike me as the noble type."

Yaz looked at Zoey with hope in his eyes. Her statement made sense. No matter what, Trish would not give up a life of comfort for anyone. If her husband were abusing her, she would have demanded more to keep her mouth shut.

"Thanks, Sassy, you gave me something to think about," he replied miserably. "See you are my calm."

Zoey hated seeing the sadness in his eyes. Yaz stopped in front of her gazing into her eyes. She wanted to turn away, but beneath his cloudy, gray eyes was just a glint of sparkle or was it the light in the room.

"Yaz, no," she whispered.

"Yes Sassy, I have to," he whispered back. Before Zoey knew it, Yaz pulled her into his arms and his lips touched hers so softly, she wasn't sure he was there.

I'm sorry I hurt you," he said against her lips.

Zoey knew she should stop him, or, at least, push him away. She did neither.

"Kiss me Yaz," she whispered back.

His mouth covered hers, wild, hot, and passionately. His tongue tasting her sweetness as she tasted his.

Zoey purred as his caressing hand stroked her back moving to cup her behind pressing her against his aroused flesh. Zoey gasped. Her heart felt ready to burst, her flipping stomach as yet to settle itself, and the unfamiliar wet thickness saturated her panties.

Yaz lips moved to her neck where it met her shoulder and her legs trembled, threatening to collapse. He lifted her and laid her on the sofa. Innocently intrigued, she gazed up at him. He needed more than just the taste of her mouth, he needed to taste the sweetness of her essences. Her eyes were glazed with wonder.

Zoey opened her mouth with the intention to put a stop to this assault on her senses, but Yaz mouth covered hers in a heated kiss, a kiss she could not stop. Instead, her arm slipped around his neck holding him to her. Her husky purr heightened his libido as his hand slipped under the jersey that covered her body to find her fevered breast. His hand brushed over the sensitive tip. Zoey sucked air through her teeth arching her back and whimpered.

Yaz smiled inside. He should have realized in this small body there would be passion. He molded and stroked his thumbs across the sensitive buds and lifted her shirt pulling it over her head. Her breasts were perfectly shaped and beautiful, and her sexy nipples looked delicious, and he could not wait, he had to taste them.

Zoey never felt anything so glorious in her life. Her hands lightly caressed his head as his hot mouth devoured her breast, making her senseless. She was torn and knew he needed to stop, but she was powerless to stop him. She heard an unfamiliar sound and realized that it was coming for her and extremely loud.

"Oh Yaz stop--no, don't stop," she moaned.

His mouth released her nipple with a soft pop, as his lips left trails of heat over her tight abs. Zoey lifted her head to see where he was leading, Her head fell back to the sofa when his hot breath blew on her panty covered treasure. Her hips lifted when his fingers traced her swollen nether lips, before slipping into the edge of her panties touching her uncharted territory. His fingers stroked her, opening her. Her breath seized when his fingers caressed her engorged nubbin.

"Please!" She groaned.

Yaz slipped her panties off, setting her in a sitting position knelt between her lifting her legs placing them on his shoulders.

"Come for me Sassy, I need to taste you, Baby." His head dipped between her legs and inhaled her unique scent, swiping his tongue slowly up her slit. Zoey's body seized.

Come for me Baby," Yaz whispered, before dipping his head again.

"I don't know how," she panted.

Yaz smiled. If he wasn't sure he was her first, he was now. He gripped her hips he lifted her to his mouth and devoured her. His tongue flicked in and out and sucked her. Her muscles seized and her thighs began to quiver. She never felt anything like this and if she had to describe it, it was as if she was on the edge of a cliff, and with one step she would fall to her death. It was both exhilarating and scary.

Yaz lifted his head. She was on the edge ready to take the leap.

"Come for me Baby, I need to taste more of your sweetness." This time, when his mouth covered her treasure, his finger eased into tight haven. She started lifting her hips frantically.

"Yaz, I...,"

"That's it Baby come for me, let me see you come," he coaxed sultrily. There it was, her first orgasm, and she was beautiful in her ecstasy and Yaz was so turned on by her passion, he climax right along with her. Yaz rose leaving a dazed but sated Zoey. He went to the bath and cleaned up while looking around her bathroom. He has never seen a bath quite like this. Everything was marble. It was unique just like Zoey.

After cleaning himself, he wets a cloth for Zoey. She lay sprawled as he left her. Gently he wiped her. He then heard her soft sigh. Damn if she didn't fall asleep. Yaz lifted her, cradling her in his arms and put her to bed. Gently he placed a kiss on her forehead. "Goodnight Baby," he whispered.

"Mm...," was all he heard.

After leaving Zoey's and since it was already Saturday and Sunday they had a home game, Yaz decided to get what rest he could, he would not be able to if he went home. So, he stayed at his Center City condo. Damn he felt good. Better than he did in a long time. Now he had to deal with Trish. He would get Satch to a little investigating for him.

It surprised Yaz to see Zoey on the field. She never mentioned she was filling in for Dr. Olivetti, who was on a much needed vacation. She was sitting a few benches down next to David. Byron Harris, the team's wide receiver, went over and sat beside her. He didn't forget Byron was all over Zoey at the party the other night. He discovered he didn't like any man talking to what was his. Whether Zoey realized it or not she was his.

Zoey was busy laughing with Byron and did not notice him, or she was just ignoring him, he thought. Yaz approached the three.

"Hey Sassy," he greeted.

Zoey looked up, her eyes straying to his mouth. That's right Baby, remember.

Her cheeks turn rosy. "Yaz can I speak with you a minute," she asked walking away.

When they were a distance away from the others, she turned to face him.

Yaz grinned. "Did you sleep well Sassy?"

Zoey's eyes narrowed. She reached up and grabbed him by his shoulder pads snatching him to her level.

"That can never happen again," she hissed before letting him go.

Yaz smiled showing his beautiful white teeth.

"Oh Sassy, it will happen again and again," he cockily assured her.

"No, it won't. I will not be the other woman!" She yelled storming off.

Yaz laughed. "Hey, Sassy?" He called. Zoey stopped and turned.

"You're the only woman!"

Zoey turned and walked away, a smile lighting her face.

Jim and Trish sat in the stands of the Stallions home game, watching the couple on the field. Jim glared at the couple.

"I thought you had him wrapped?" He complained.

"How can I when he is never at home," she whined.

"Did you, at least, talk about me to him," Jim asked irritated.

"I tried but he said he did not want to hear your name in his house again."

"Damn it, I got to get back to him. Calvin and his aunt gave up."

"Maybe you ought to also," Trish advised.

"Never! He wouldn't be where he is without me. I made him."

"What are you going to do?" Trish whined in that sickening southern accent.

Jim glared at the woman beside him. She got what she wanted, she got Yaz Bryant and his money. If she's not careful, she could lose too.

"First I have to get rid of that bitch," he growled.

The game was in full swing and Zoey being an avid Stallion's fan was on the sidelines with Coach Singleton yelling as much as he was. David glanced at Zoey and smiled.

"You like him don't you, Little Bit?"

"Who?" Zoey frowned up at him.

"Yaz Bryant, Stallions star running back," he stated grinning.

"No, I do not, but if he gets hurt out there today I'm going to hurt him even more," she warned.

David chuckled. "They gotta stop him first and if they let him slip by, he's gone," David said with pride. "They only got three points up on us," he said watching the game. David was the only team owner she knew that was on the field every game. "There he goes!" David exclaimed, running up the sideline waving his arms wildly.

As soon as he crossed the goal line for the touchdown he was hit hard with body crashing down on him. The fans were on their feet cheering while the referees were in the mix pulling players off. Yaz lay face down on the field and was too still for Zoey liking.

"Give him a minute," Zoey murmured to herself, wringing her hands as her heart hammered in her chest. She watched as the trainers ran out to the field.

"We need you Doc," someone said through the headpiece she wore. Zoey ran out to the field, with the cart following behind her. She fell to her knees over him, pressing a stethoscope into his back. She moved close to his ear. "Don't you dare be hurt Yaz or you will live to regret it," she whispered.

"Yaz! Zoey shouted.

His eyes flickered open.

"Roll him over," she ordered. Zo leaned over to check his eyes. They were dazed and unclear, not a good sign.

"Yaz, where are you?" He blinked again.

"YAZ!!!"

"Will you stop that damn shouting Sassy, my head is throbbing." he moaned.

Zoey exhaled with relief. "Load him up fellas," she ordered.

Zoey climbed in beside him and glared down at him. "If you would stop showing off you would have prevented this injury," she scolded.

"Showing off? I just ran a touchdown. How is that showing off?" He questioned, despite the hammering in his head.

"I'm just saying," she countered and rolled her eyes.

Nag, nag, nag," Yaz grinned and Zoey could not help smiling back.

Yaz and Zoey were in the training room checking his vitals. His eyes were still a little cloudy, which concerned her.

"Can I go back in the game Doc?"

"The game just ended and the Stallions took the game 31-24. Your TD did it. I'm proud of you," she whispered.

"Can you kiss my boo-boo?" Yaz smiled mischievously.

"Stop that Yaz."

"I promise it will make me feel better," he pouted.

"You are hopeless." She chuckled.

"Yaz! Yaz! Are you alright?" Trish came rushing into the training room.

Zoey turned blocking Yaz.

"You cannot come in here!" she told her frowning.

"He is my fiancée. I want to know how he is," she said trying to sound worried as she glared at Zoey. She ignored Zoey and Trish tried to push her out of the way. Zoey did not budge.

"Look, leave quietly or security will remove you, Belle," Zoey warned her arms folded across to chest stubbornly.

"Go home Trish," Yaz spoke up.

"Are you alright honey? If anything happened...,"

"You got until three to get out," Zoey interrupted.

"Yazy," she whined. "You have to stop playing or you are going to get seriously hurt and then who will I have to take care of me?"

"Two ... Three. Security come down to the training room, please!"

"Yazy, I want to stay," she whined.

"You can't. Go home Trish," Yaz sounding exasperated.

Two burly security guards entered the room. "Okay lady lets go."

"When will you be home?" Trish whined. Yaz remained silent.

Zoey shook her head at them as Trish was led from the room. "You sure know how to pick um," she commented. "I'm going to check you in the hospital. You have a concussion. How severe I don't know, but to be on the safe side, I want to take a few tests."

"Hospital? Come on Doc!"

"I want to be on the safe side, so stop whining."

Duke and Satch then entered the room grinning. "Are you alright Yaz?

Great game MVP," Satch grinned.

Yaz tried to smile but grimaced.

"Don't congratulate him for showing off."

"Showing off?" Duke and Satch echoed incredulously.

"They will be showing that play for months which gives you unlimited choices next season, I'm sure David's not letting you go, which gives us the upper hand. You could...,"

"Out you two! No business now, Duke," Zoey ordered.

It was useless to argue with Zoey. "Who made her so bossy?" Satch asked as they left the room.

After being transported to the hospital and the tests were completed, Zoey ordered a mild pain reliever for his headache. While Yaz lay asleep, she sat beside the bed studying his face.

"Oh Yaz, I tried not loving you, but I can help it," she whispered. Her hand lightly smoothed a frown from his brow. She kissed him gently on a forehead.

"Trish," he murmured.

Zoey sighed dejectedly. Even sedated he thought of her. "You are a fool, Zola Ella Howard," she whispered leaving the room.

Three weeks later Yaz sat with the brothers each looking glum.

"You found out something?" Yaz asked.

"Yes," Satch replied.

"Well?" Yaz prompted.

It seems Trish Devereaux Beaufort was not a victim of spousal abuse. Congressman Beaufort divorced his wife due to infidelity. Although it is true, she has nothing, due to the prenuptial contract if she is caught in an extramarital affair she loses all monies and properties. She is known to be associated with Jim Bailey, and as early as yesterday they were photographed together. Her parents are destitute and has shunned her because of her scandalous behavior and is an embarrassment to their circle of friends. In layman's terms Yaz, you have been lied to you again.

Yaz blood began to boil.

"I went one step further, I had Jim Bailey investigated too. It seems Jim had accepted gifts in your mother's name when you were being scouted. It was also confirmed that the Bueto's refused to negotiate with him without you being present because they said he wanted a finder's fee written into the contract."

"What?"

Jim had promised Mississippi State University you would attend their school for a gift of 50 grand. The scouts said your mother even met with them. The investigator showed the man a picture of your mother and one of your aunt. It would appear your Aunt Margaret posed as your mother. Satch glanced at Duke.

Yaz, I need you to remain calm while he finishes." Duke advised.

"Remain calm!" He shouted. "What more could there be!"

"There is more," Satch commented. Yaz agreed.

"When you did not attend MSU the rogue scout contacted your mother demanding the money be returned. We think, and this is only speculation that your mother confronted Jim."

"If she felt something was wrong I know she confronted him. And, then two weeks later my mother was mugged." Yaz completed.

Was Jim responsible for his mother's death Yaz wondered? Yaz was deathly quiet. Muggings happened every day to some unsuspecting individuals. But this was too much of a consequence.

The brothers saw his hands trembling when he lifted them. He looked at each of them.

"You think...,"

"We don't know; we put our investigators on it." They will find and question everyone who knows or has had business dealings with Jim Bailey along with his legal and illegal associates.

Yaz was on his feet his gray eyes stormy. "If he is responsible for my mother's death, I swear I'm going to kill him!" Yaz shouted.

"No," he whispered. "No, no, no!" His head dropped.

"Send in Zoey," Duke spoke into the intercom.

Zoey walked next to Yaz tense body at the table.

"Yaz," she spoke softly touching the fisted hand that was pressed the table.

His head lifted slowly to acknowledge her, tears streaming down his handsome face.

"Sassy," he croaked. "They killed her, I feel it." He faced Zoey and fell to his knees his face pressed into a middle, his arms wrapped around her waist holding her close.

Zoey looked at her brothers sadly, tipping her head towards the door motioning for them to leave them alone. Zoey soothingly caressed his head until his tears subsided and he came to his feet. The murderous look on Yaz's face calls Zoey to steps back.

"If I see them, I will not hesitate to hurt them," he threatened, and Zoey had no doubt by his words.

Zoey looked directly into his eyes. "Yaz, do you trust me?"

"Yes, I do."

"Then come with me and asked no questions."

In Cherry Hill, Trish sat across from Jim in a restaurant. "What the hell do you mean Yaz has not been home in three weeks?" Jim asked harshly. "You were supposed to wrap him around your finger. What the hell happened?"

Trish face turned red. "Jim something's wrong, and I want to get out of town," Trish whined.

"Not yet. If Calvin is watching the doctor like I told him, we will know where they are."

"What are you doing, spying on her?"

"You want her out of the way don't you?" Trish nodded.

"Trust me; I know where she is as we speak, "Jim boasted. Trish looked skeptical. Things are not working out how as she thought they would be. Trish really thought she could wrap Yaz around a finger as she had in the past, but nothing is working out how she wanted, and she was going to wind up back in New Orleans was nothing.

Jim took out his phone. The phone rang picking up voice mail. Jim cursed.

"Give me a couple of days. If nothing develops, I will take you to the Airport myself."

Chapter 12

On the drive to wherever Zoey was taking him, Yaz remained mind numbing silent. Did Jim and Calvin have something to do with his mother's death? Jim was the only father figure he had known and he has always been devoted to him. Always interested in his life and in the direction it was going. He knew his mom was not fond of it Jim, and on many occasions, she advised him to be careful. That was the only time he got extremely upset with his mother when she shared her thoughts about Jim. After the argument, her parting words were only "all that glitters is not gold Son. All I want is for you to be happy and satisfied with life. And, always know I love you and come hell or high water I will protect you with my life." She then left his room.

Zoey also recognized Jim not to be an honest man after only meeting him a couple of times. Was he so gullible that he could not see Jim for the man he truly was? His cousin Calvin, he was not surprised. He already knew since childhood Calvin and Aunt Margaret never cared for him and his mother. There was nothing new there. If what the Howard brothers thought was true, and his mother confronted Jim, which he was sure she did, did Jim get scared that she would report him? Yet, Satch said they had no proof, but that did not mean he did not have a motive. Jim had taken bribes and made promises to schools he would have never considered attending. Was he so greedy that he took his mother's life to shut her up?

Even though, it happened five years ago, his mother's death still haunted him. Then, there was Trish Devereaux, the devastatingly beautiful woman that was hideous on the inside, which now was starting to show through, and again he fell for her lies. It was too much. Tears stung the backs of his eyes and he shut them tight grinding the heel of his hands into them. He wanted answers and he wanted them now. Tears seeped down his face, his breathing now deep and harsh.

Zoey glanced at Yaz when a harsh breath escaped him. She could see the tears of despair leak from his eyes and her heart broke for him. They were almost at Duke's condo in center city. When they got there, she would talk to him and convince him that going after Jim was not the way to go. Her heart literally ached for him as she watched the hurt, confusion, and despair so plainly in his gray orbs. She yearned to take him in her arms and comfort him until he felt nothing but her love for him.

Yaz looked out the window unseeingly at the pedestrian moving up the congested Broad Street. He knew Zoey saw the frustrated tears streaming down his face yet he was not ashamed. If there was anyone he could have an emotional collapse with, it was with Zoey; his calm. To think he shunned her for Trish and like his mother said all that glitters is not gold. The anger inside him needed to be unleashed, and he needed to unleash it on Jim. Then, he would get rid of that manipulating evil Trish for the last time.

"Take me to Jim!" Yaz growled at Zoey.

"Nope!" She replied. Zoey pulled in front of the valet stand and put the car in park.

Yaz eyes narrowed. "I'm not asking you, Zola, I'm telling you," he countered remaining in the car as she got out. Yaz watched as she moved to hand the valet her keys. While she took a moment to check in, he remained where he was. Zoey turned to face the car where he still sat. A frown creased her brow her and with her fists on her shapely hips glared at him, she went to the car snatching open the car door. Yaz folded his arms across his broad chest stubbornly.

"Get out of that car Yazair!" She ordered.

"Take me to see Jim," he countered.

"No!" She replied through tight lips.

"You will take me now Zoey. This is not a game!"

"Mr. Bryant you have two options, you get out the car on your own or I will have you dragged out."

"That's no option Zoey. You will get that fine ass in this car and drive me to Voorhees, and if you are wondering this is not a request!" He shouted.

"Well, I have it on excellent authority that the twins and your teammates Queszal and Troy live in the penthouse two floors below Duke.

Was this girl crazy? "What the hell is your point?" Yaz yelled exasperated.

Zoey ignored him and casually scrolled down the contacts in her phone. She pressed the call button humming as she waited for someone to connect.

Yaz cursed under his breath. He needed her because he left his car at the office, and Jim lived in Voorhees. If Zoey still refused to take him, he would hail a cab no matter the cost and have it take him to Voorhees. Yaz glanced over at Zoey blocking his way and rolled his eyes.

"Hey Quez, it's Zoey. I have a large package that needs to be delivered to Duke's. I'm downstairs, thanks.

Zoey smiled smugly at Yaz.

"Move Zola now!" Yaz growled.

Move me," she challenged.

Yaz pushed open the passenger door and slid out towering over Zoey just as the enormous twins Queszal and Troy stepped behind her.

Zoey looked over her shoulder at the large men behind her.

"Yaz, Zoey," they both greeted.

"Hello fellas," she spoke to the twins, her eyes still on Yaz.

"Queszal, Troy, I have a large package to deliver, and it seems I cannot get it upstairs. Could you help?"

"Anything for you little sister no questions asked," Troy said.

Yaz frowned. Was Zoey related to these two characters?

"I need you to take Yaz up to Duke's, if he resists, knock him out."

"What the..., Knock me out..., Look...," Yaz sputtered.

"Yaz, I'm sure you don't want to make a scene in the busy hustle and bustle of Center City do you?" She asked politely.

"I don't give a damn about Center City right now I need to get to Voorhees Zoey. Now!"

"Okay, I warned you."

Yaz looked from Zoey to the Zeus-sized men behind her. He stared at Zoey incredulously. Now his anger was explosive. He bent forward just as Zoey moved aside and ran into the brick walls; that is all he remembered.

His eyes fluttered open to a warm cloth caressing his face. As his vision cleared and seeing the beautiful tawny face, Yaz mouth curled slightly upward. He was upset with Zoey and her bossy ways, but he still couldn't help admiring her. Who was he trying to fool, damn it; she was precious to him.

Yaz pulled the cloth from her hand and tried to rise. She pushed him back.

"Go for the drama much?" He replied sarcastically.

"Stubborn much?" She countered.

"Why Zoey?"

Zoey shrugged. "Duke wants me to keep you out of trouble, and he also said that will not bail you out of jail. So he asked me to keep you occupied.

Yaz had to smile. He knew of only one way he wanted to be kept busy with her. To control his wayward thoughts and body, he asked. "What would you have done in my place Zoey?

"Oh, Duke understands, and more than likely he would do exactly what you are contemplating, but that will only make matters worse."

Yaz knew they were right. "So how do you propose to keep me busy and not go after Jim, Calvin and Trish?"

Zoey eyes lowered. She knew what she wanted and what she craved. She wanted to feel that fires she felt the other night after the dance.

"I don't know, but you are not leaving this place until we hear from Duke." Zoey rose from the side of the bed. "Hungry?"

"No!" He said gruffly.

"Too bad, you are going to eat if I have to shove it down your throat." Zoey turned and left the room.

Calvin paced the sparsely furnished study waiting for Jim. Why did he let Jim talk him into this shit? Now he was over his head, and his Mama was a part of it. They should have been happy with the house Yaz bought them liberating them from the ghetto of West Philly. But no, mama wanted more. She wanted Yaz to take care of them by giving them a larger monthly allowance. What he gave was not enough, according to his mother. Right now neither had to work, but Mama wanted more.

He has hated Yaz ever since his mother took them in fourteen years ago after his father died. Yaz was everything he was not. He was smart, good-looking, popular, and skilled in everything he did, and a mother that supported him in all his interests. Not like his mother who was all about herself, only interested in what was in it for her? Sometimes he couldn't believe they were twins. It was not long before Aunt Martha found a teaching job, and they moved to a bigger better house out of the ghetto.

Yaz soon began playing football in high school and was the toast of Philly. Calvin wanted that glory. Whenever he opened the paper, all he saw was the triumph of Yaz Bryant, All-Star Penn State Heisman Trophy winner. Now a pro, he was still just as talented if not better. MVP for the two years he played with the Atlanta Buetos, and then when he came to Philly to play for the Stallions his first year he was nominated MVP nationally. Yaz was generous enough, but he wanted what Yaz had. His hatred grew along with his mother's greed.

During his last year in high school, he was considered a blue chip player to colleges and universities around the country. The offers from the finest colleges and universities were staggering. Even with his popularity, Yaz turned down all other colleges and universities that were interested in him, having promised his mother he would stay in Pennsylvania and attend Penn State. Jim was not happy with Yaz's choice but failed to convince Aunt Martha and Yaz to consider other offers. The mistake Jim made was accepting a gift from a group of men from Mississippi that had a hand in the college football pool, and knowing full well Yaz would not be attending their colleges. That was one gift Jim could not resist. He couldn't get Yaz's mother to help him convince Yaz to attend MSU, so he enlisted the help of his mother to pretend to be Aunt Martha to get a piece of the twenty grand Jim would receive. Unfortunately, before Yaz graduated from Penn State the shady individuals called Aunt Martha demanding she return the money she knew nothing about. Aunt Martha confronted Jim ordering him to fix that problem or she would tell Yaz just how sleazy his Manager actually is, not to mention reporting him to the NCAA along with the men involved. She was not going to allow Jim to ruin her son's career by involving him in his illegal dealings. The NCAA frowns on players taking bribes and gifts, and those powerful men told him that if he did not stop her, they would shut him up. With the offer of a grand, Jim convinced him to find out when and where his Aunt Martha would be alone. Next thing he knew Aunt Martha was dead and Yaz was on any downward spiral leaving everything to the care of Jim until that sports doctor came along pulling him from his destructive ways. Jim is convinced she is the reason for his turnaround. He was sure she was the one who introduced Yaz to the Howard Brothers Consulting firm. Now with Trish in the picture, it has gotten more out of control. A couple of days ago an investigator started asking questions about Jim and his connection to Aunt Martha.

The shit was about to hit the fan and his Mama had hightailed it down to Tennessee, leaving him to deal with Jim's shit. He should have gone with her.

Where in the hell was Jim he wondered looking at the door. If he didn't show in the next five minutes, he was going to haul ass out of there and join his mother in Tennessee. Calvin growled before sitting on the leather sofa.

"What's up and make it quick, I'm an extremely busy man."

"There has been some investigator coming around asking questions about Aunt Martha mugging."

Jim shrugged. "So, as far as I'm concerned it was a random thing."

"Yeah, but the man that was questioning Mama asked about this sports group from Mississippi. He claimed to report them to the NCAA out of Mississippi has a known group of men that offer gifts to convince potential blue chip players to go to MSU. Then, he asked what me and Mama knew about the mugging. When he finished questioning Mama, he also informed her anyone involved could be possibly arrested as an accomplice."

"What?" Jim roared.

"That's why I came over here, Mama has gone down South.

"She's what? Didn't she know that will only make us look guilty?"

"What do you mean us?" Calvin shouted coming to his feet. "I didn't have anything to do with that. That was you and Mama's scam."

"Maybe so, but you are involved my boy. Don't forget you stalked your Aunt and told me her every move. You are in it just by association," Jim stated calmly.

"Hell no!" Calvin cried shaking his head. "I didn't mug her; your boy did that."

"Yeah, it was unfortunate that she died. I'd told that asshole to just scare her, and tell her to keep her mouth shut. He claims she fought taking off his ski masks. Said he had to kill her because she saw his face.

Calvin threw up his hands. "I'm done with this shit. It's out of control. First, you have my aunt killed; now you got me following that doctor. What you gonna do have her killed too?"

"I did not want Martha dead, just quieted. But that smart mouth bitch has messed up my good thing and for that matter, you and your mother has too. I don't want her dead, I want what she stole from me. She interfered with my business, and now I'm screwed. I thought Trish was going to get Yaz to take me back, but she failed in that too. So I have to take matters into my own hands.

"Fine, whenever, I'm done. I don't want to know nothing." Calvin turned to leave. Before he could get through the open door, the next words stopped him in his tracks.

"Oh no my boy," Jim replies sinisterly. "You and your mama are up in this to your eyeballs." Calvin turned and glared at Jim.

"No Jim, you're wrong. All I did was follow Aunt Martha and maybe take money, but I had nothing to do with killing her."

Jim waved his hand in the air nonchalantly. "You see son, they have no description of the culprit that mugged Martha. An anonymous call can fix all that, and with the alleged $100 grand reward for info..., well let's just say Calvin, my boy your ass will be grass, along with your mother."

Calvin's heart began to beat painfully in his chest.

"If I go down, it will not be for the unfortunate death of Martha Bryant. What will I get five years or less for embezzlement? You, my boy, will get life," Jim sneered. "Now sit your ass down and listen and do as I say and all will be well."

Yaz didn't have much of an appetite, but he ate something just to appease the beautiful, sassy miss sitting across from him. Damn, how he admired Zola Howard. She was everything a man or this man would want, he realized. At one time, he thought he wanted a woman fawn all over him, and let him spoil her, in other words, mindless and shallow was what he wanted and that was Trish Devereaux. Zoey was not only strong but intelligent and she made him laugh. Hell, she made him happy. However, right now all he wanted was to confront Jim and his family. He needed to believe they didn't have anything to do with his mother's tragic death. His patience was wearing very thin.

"I am ready to leave," Yaz grunted.

"Nope." Zo took a bite of her sandwich, ignoring him.

"You can't keep me here Zola," he replied getting pissed as he came to his feet, moving from the table.

"Yes, you're right, but I think until more is known about Jim you ought to stay put," she advised, rising from the table to stand in front of him.

Screw that, Yaz thought. "I do appreciate what you and your brothers are trying to do Zoey, but I'm leaving," he said moving around her

Zoey frowned. What now, what could she do to stop him? Tell him how you feel and what you want, her mind screamed.

Zoey pulled the T-shirt over her head exposing her lacy peach bra. She knew nothing about seducing a man, but this was a start.

"Yaz," Zoey called hoping her tone was seductive.

Yaz turned. His eyes drank in her partially nude body. Her perfect breasts covered in peach lace, appreciating the curve of her waist and the tight muscles of her abs.

His eyes narrowed. "Put your clothes on Zola, he ordered. "I'm sure your brothers didn't mean for you to strip just to keep me here." He turned continuing out of the room.

Zoey was mortified. Hot tears stung the backs of her eyes. She slipped her shirt on Yaz headed for the door. Fine, if he wanted to go he could, she thought. She blinked rapidly trying to stem the tears that threatened to fall. Yaz was just reaching for the doorknob when she spoke.

"Fine Yaz, if you want to be a stubborn moron that's on you, we thought we were helping you. And, for the record you are right, my brothers would not appreciate me using those tactics to keep you here. For some ungodly, reason I fell in love and wanted only to give myself to you. Sorry, I don't have the finesse of your Southern Belle...," Zoey paused, her throat seemed to clog and her eyes started burning again. "Go Mr. Bryant, find Jim and your no account family confront them with what you know, I don't care. Tears now flowed down her cheeks. "Let them get the upper hand if they don't have it already, I don't care!" Zoey turned moving swiftly away from him.

Yaz followed and reached out grasping her upper arm to stop her. "What did you say?" He asked stunned.

Zoey snatched her arm free. "Go to hell, moron!" She cried quickly moving away.

Yaz rushed after her catching her around the waist pulling her into him.

"Let me go!" She hissed struggling against him.

"Sassy," he whispered before taking her lobe into his warm mouth.

Zoey stiffened, even though her eyes shut dreamily. Yaz turned her into his embrace his smoky gray eyes met her dark ones.

"You love me?" Yaz said in a deep sexy tone and Zoey was lost in his sexy eyes.

"Say it again, Sassy?" He coaxed smoothly as he pulled her closer to him.

"No, never again," she whispered her eyes looking at his mouth with undisguised longing. Yaz head lowered and gently touched his lips to hers. Zoey softly moaned and her eyes slowly closed. Her arms slid around his shoulders and closed around his neck while her body melted in his arm. Tongues battled and tasted as his hand caressed down her waist cupping her butt. It was all too much for Zoey. The sensations of his mouth and hands had her entire body pulsating. She felt that indescribable thickness between her legs and pleasure in the pit of her stomach.

Yaz swung her up in his arms his lips still covering hers as he moved to the guest bedroom. Without breaking contact with her mouth, Yaz followed her down on the bed on top of her. His head lifted and he looked into her dark, sensual eyes.

"If we go here, there will be no turning back Zola, you will be mine now forever do you understand."

She sighed nodding her head. She loved him so much and at this point she didn't care that he didn't say the words. He wanted her and that was enough for now. Zoey felt his hands lifting her shirt and she helped by raising her arms as he pulled it over her head tossing it to the floor. While he unbuttoned her jeans, she unbuttoned his shirt. Although she has seen his beautiful body many times, it still awed her at how perfect he is. Once his shirt was discarded Zoey rose up on her elbows and did what she'd been dying to do for a long time. She pressed her lips to his sculptured chest tasting him. Her small hands caressed him as her mouth trailed hot kisses. Zoey heard him moan and she smiled.

Yaz lay her back on the bed. "Lift up, Sassy," he whispered.

Zoey's hips rose as Yaz slip pants and panties down her legs and over her already bare feet.

Yaz grunted. She was bare, how sexy that is, he thought.

Misinterpreting his response, Zoey tried to pull away. Yaz stopped her retreat. When he tasted her before she had a small amount of hair, now she was completely bald. Yaz smiled seductively. "Is this for me?" He asked as his finger caressed down her center.

Zoey gasped but otherwise remain silent. His hands slowly caressed her rounded hips to her small waist stopping at her rib cage. With the flick of his wrist, Yaz opened the front closure of her bra. Air sucked through Yaz's teeth at the sight of her beautiful breasts that sat high on her chest full with hard dark nipples. Yaz could not resist, he took one of those perky buds in his mouth. Zoey moaned and grasped the duvet in her fists. Yaz switched his hot mouth covering her other breast. Zoey moaned and held him to her breast as he sucked and nipped at her.

Reluctantly Yaz pulled away rising and removing his pants. Zoey's eyes widened. She knew he was impressive, but damn. There was no way he would fit inside her, yet she was intrigued enough to try it. It was time to tell Yaz she has never done this before.   "Yaz,

I've never ...,"

Yaz pressed his finger to her lips. "I know Sassy if you want to stop...,"

"No, no, I want this. I want you only...,"

Yaz interrupted by covering her mouth in a deep passionate kiss. He then realized how honored he was to be her first and definitely her only. He has wasted enough time plus he wanted Zoey as his. He wanted to be hers and after tonight, she would be his mind, body, and soul.

Yaz trailed hot kisses to her neck marking her as his; he traveled lower her overly sensitive nipples. When his mouth found its way to her treasure, Zoey moaned loudly. Yaz tasted, licked and sucked her sensitive nub of with his tongue. Pressure began to build in her lower body and her thighs began to tremble when Yaz introduced one finger into her tight sheath. She moaned as he sucked and caressed her. When he slipped another finger, she screamed his name moving wildly beneath him.

She was ready. Yaz held her hips lifting her so when she exploded he could take all of her essences. He could feel it, she was right on the edge and ready to tumble over. Yaz tongue pushed into her and Zoey exploded screaming his name as he feasted on her.

When she calmed, Yaz moved up to cover her body. "Yaz," she moaned. "I never felt like that before."

"It's only just begun sweetheart." Yaz cursed; no condoms He has never gone without a condom even with Trish. He was healthy and he knew Zoey was too. When he remained still above her, Zoey wondered why.

"Yaz?" She whispered tentatively.

Yaz looked into her eyes. "You trust me Sassy?"

"Yes..., Yes I do," She answered.

"You trust me?" Zoey countered.

"More than you know baby," he replied before his mouth and body covered hers.

Yaz parted her legs, gently pushing into her.

"Oh baby," he moaned when her walls clasped and her moisture surrounded him. Slowly he eased into her. Yaz sucked air when her tight sheath literally sucked him in. He would not be able to hold on much longer.

"Zoey, look at me," Yaz ordered huskily. Her eyes opened.

"I'm going to take you now; it's going to hurt...,"

"Do it Yaz, please, I need...,"

Before she can say another word, Yaz broke through the barrier implanting himself inside her. He stilled giving her time to adjust to the fullness of him. Although it was killing him, he would wait until she made the first move. It didn't take long, her bottom flexed, and he met her. It wasn't long before their bodies were in sync with the other. When Yaz would retreat Zoey was there with lifted hips ready to receive him in her tight body. The pressure was beginning to build within the sensuous moaning couple. Zoey felt like she was ready to ignite and Yaz never wanted to leave her tight cocoon.

"Yes, yes!" Zoey moaned lifting her hips to meet his thrust. Their bodies moved faster and Zoey begged for him to help her. Yaz rose to his knees lifting her hips and held her still as he moved pumping and gyrating in her until she exploded, drenching him with her hot essence sparking his orgasm. Never had he felt like this. Zoey had marked him and she was his.

Yaz rolled off pulling her into his arms

"Oh my," Zoey sighed awe-filled and breathless. "That was so wonderful."

Yaz grinned. Yes, it was he thought, looking forward to the many more wonderful nights. He could never let her go now.

Zoey moved closer into Yaz before she settled and he knew she had fallen asleep.

Yaz gently eased from the bed. It was time to take care of his business. He knew Duke would be furious, but he had to find out what happened with his mother and then he had to clean his house.

Now dressed, Yaz gently kissed Zoey's forehead before leaving and he called a cab to take him to get his car, and from there he was going to Jim's house in Voorhees. Twenty minutes later he arrived at Jim's deserted house. Next he went to Aunt Margaret's house again it seemed to be deserted as well. Yaz sat in his car. Calvin should be coming in soon. After sitting an hour, Yaz pulled out his cell phone and dialed Calvin's number. It went a voice mail.

"If I were you, Calvin, it would be a good thing if you called me back ASAP!" Yaz clicked off. He glanced at his watch it was after midnight and it was time to clean his house.

114

Yaz let himself into his house taking the stairs two at the time. As he moved closer to the door, he heard heavy breathing and moans. He pushed open the door find Trish's wildly riding some dude in his bed. Trish's screamed and fell off the bed. The dude she was riding looked at him visibly surprised and shaken.

"Hey man, she told me she was divorced and single," he said scrambling to get out of bed.

"Just get dressed and get the hell out my house, and take her with you!" Yaz ordered.

Trish rose with the sheet wrapped around there. "Yaz you can't...,"

"Oh, but I can!" He snapped.

"Hey man, I can't take her with me, my wife...,"

"Get out!" Yaz roared.

Buck naked, the man scooped up his clothes and headed for the door. Trish sat on the side of the bed tears running down her face. Yaz looked at her with disgust.

"Get dressed Trish!"

"What was I supposed to do? You never came home."

"First of all, this is not your home and never will be. Do you think I'm so in love with you that I would allow you to walk all over me? I'm a man Trish, a man you thought you were too good for back then. Then, after all, these years, you decide you love, the black man that was just your pet.

Trish gasped. "I'd told you, I said that just to pacify my mother."

"Save it!" Yaz roared. "You are only going to fool me once, Trish. I know you lied about your husband of abusing you. He divorced you for the same thing I caught you doing. I know Jim brought you here to talk me into taking him back. By the way, where is Jim?"

"I don't know," sounding desperate. "Yaz, you can't just put me out. I don't have anywhere to go."

"Go back to New Orleans, to your broke ass, stuck up parents. Now you got thirty minutes to get your shit and get out. A taxi is going to take you to a hotel and your plane ticket will be at the airport."

Yaz turned to leave. "You have thirty minutes," he replied over his shoulder.

Trish stared dumbfounded at his retreating back as tears coursed down her face, this time, they were real tears. Yaz was her last hope for happiness. First, she ruined her marriage to

Beaufort, now she lost Yaz. She wiped tears from her eyes. She was beautiful and she will find another man to worship and take care of her. She pulled out her luggage and packed all her favorite things she purchased.

Thirty minutes later Yaz was putting Trish in a taxi directing him to take her to the hotel he reserved for her. Trish sat in the back seat of the cab with her head down. Yaz looked at her, her head rose, and her eyes met his.

"Yaz, please."

Yaz shook his head. "Goodbye, Trish."

Chapter 13

Jim sat in his car watching as Yaz pulled into his driveway. Where the hell had he been? A couple of weeks after Yaz brought Trish home he left and did not return and, of course, Trish whined, as if he would care. She was not holding up her end of the bargain. She was supposed to make Yaz fall in love with her and then convince him to take him back. He just needed to warn her about how things are now going. Too late Yaz finally came back home.

Thankful for the darkness Jim watched from a safe distance. He wouldn't be able to sit here long because the police patrolled this predominantly wealthy white neighborhood around the clock. Jim's eyebrows rose to his hairline, a smirk on his face. Shaking his head, he chuckled. A partially nude man was running up the street to a parked car. So Trish got busted again. A few minutes later a yellow cab pulled in the driveway. Trish and her luggage were being loaded inside. Oh well, Trish was one headache he was glad to be rid of. Jim watched as Yaz turned to go into the house. There was nothing he can do now. Jim pulled from the curb. It was time to put his last plan into to action and Calvin better hope that he comes through, or they will be looking for his body. Jim dialed Calvin's number. "Calvin where's the doctor?"

Jim slammed on his brakes in the middle of the deserted street. "What the hell do you mean you lost her?" Jim shouted into the phone, moving to put Calvin on speaker.

"My boy said about noon he followed her after she left the Howard offices. He said traffic was tight and he lost her," Calvin explained.

"You are just now telling me you and your boys lost her since noon?" He yelled.

"When she left the building she was with Yaz," my boy said."

"Well, she was not with him now. I just left Yaz's place he is definitely alone, damn," Jim swore. "Go to her office, stay there, and don't let her out of your sight. You lose her, this time, Calvin, I'm calling the hotline. How does this sound, NEPHEW KILLS AUNT! When she is alone, you call me." Jim ended the call.

Yaz slipped back in the bed, pulling Zoey into his body. He was glad she slept while he was out. If she knew, there would be hell to pay.

"Did you take care of what you needed?" A sleepy Zoey asked.

"Sassy....," Yaz paused.

She wiggled her body against his, her bare behind grazing his semi-erection. He was hard the minute he had returned knowing Zoey's delectable body was in bed waiting for him. Zoey turned to face him their eyes met.

"Sassy," he said softly.

"Did you do what needed to be done?" Zoey repeated.

Yaz's eyes strayed to her sensual mouth.

"Yaz, did you?"

"Yes Sassy I did," he answered his mouth absently gently caressing her cheek.

"Good!" She replied and seemed genuinely pleased.

Yaz eyebrows dipped. "That's it," Yaz asked incredulously waiting for a lecture.

"Yes, that's it," she smiled as she traced the contours of his handsome face again realizing how deep her love was for this man. She moved closer touching her lips softly to his.

"Open for me Sassy, I need to taste you."

Yaz covered her mouth, her lips parted and he drank his fill while his hand caressed and circled her sensitive nub. He rolled her to her back wedging himself between her thighs.

A purred escaped her throat when she felt his gentle fingers caressing and stimulated nub.

He needed no more encouragement and sank into her hot moist body, welcoming him.

She clamped around him almost making him spill himself prematurely. She felt exquisite and her heart belongs to him.

Her body arched into him. That's how he loved her response to him. It was amazing how

117

uninhibited she was with her sensuality, and he loved it, and would never get enough of it.

"Yaz please," she moaned.

His grasp her hips making it impossible for her to move. Yaz gave her what he knew they both needed, moving inside her in ways he didn't know he could. His manhood touched her womb and he took her fast and hard while her head rolled wildly on the pillow and her nails dug into his biceps as she bucked beneath him.

Concentrating on her body, Yaz needed to slow down so he can give her the most mind shattering pleasure.

"Don't tease me," she whimpered.

"Look at me," he ordered huskily. Passion glazed eyes melded with his. He found himself falling into the depths of her warm chocolate eyes.

"Tell me what you want Baby?" He asked as she moved slowly to and fro matching his sensual pants, his manhood embedded deeply inside. Her walls clamp down around him and he knew she was ready to let go.

"Hard, fast, now Yaz," she moaned.

Yaz slipped his hands under her, holding her aloft as he plunged into her wet, tight body. Concentrating on her body wanting to learn what gave her the most mind shattering pleasure. One pump and she fell apart screaming his name as she milked his seed from him. They held on to each other in their sensual bliss slowly eased from their slick exhausted bodies.

Yaz tried to roll from Zoey, but she held on to him tightly.

"Baby?" Yaz whispered.

"I don't want this to end," she whispered, as her arms fell away.

"It won't, you are mine now Zoey."

Zoey looked deep into his smoky gray eyes. How she wanted to believe him. She was not beautiful or glamorous like his Southern Belle or some of the other women he dated. She was short, curvy and lack sophistication. She was sometimes brassy and definitely mouthy. She guessed being raised by five brothers made her little bolder and she didn't suffer fools kindly. It was okay right now to be with him. What about a couple of months from now, when the newness wore out. She knew she didn't want to hurt as she did when he brought the Southern Belle home with him. If he left her this time and because of their intimacy, she would never recover. Yaz sighed and rolled from her pulling her close into his body, his arms tightening around her as he fell asleep.

Zoey lay quietly beside him listening to his soft snore. It was just after 5:00 AM and she needed to get going. Yaz would be leaving for the stadium soon for the Monday night game in Atlanta. She was not ready to face him yet. At least not when she had doubts yet she had no regrets. How could she? She gave herself willingly to the man she fell in love with. Whatever happened she would never regret the time they shared. Zoey's rolled from the bed glancing back to Yaz to make sure he still slept. She gathered her clothes and quietly left the penthouse.

Zoey went straight to her office. She had been disregarding her practice since meeting Yazair Bryant, thank goodness she had a strong, loyal staff and colleagues that would fill in for her at any time. However, it was time to get back to business. Opening the door, Zoey tossed her purse on the leather sofa in her office continuing on in her bathroom for a shower and change into regular work clothes.

Now cleaned of all traces of Yaz, Zoey sat at a desk and began going over patient files stacked in her 'to do box'. At seven o'clock it was odd, but she wasn't tired, just kind of rejuvenated. Zoey smiled. Would it be like this every time she wondered? Zoey visibly shook herself. "Don't start wool-gathering Zola Ella Howard you have played around long enough," she chided herself and open the first folder.

At eight o'clock her phone vibrated at her side. Unclipping it she looked at the caller name. It was Yaz. Zoey sighed she was not ready to deal with this. She knew she had to think this through before she jumped in with both feet.

"Good morning," she said cheerfully putting him on speaker.

"Why are you not in bed?" Yaz asked grumpily.

"Because, I have an obligation to my patients. I have neglected my practice long enough."

"I understand Sassy, but it's so early in the morning," he commented.

"And...?"

"I thought maybe you might be my breakfast," he said seductively.

Instantly Zoey's panties were wet. "Yaz, don't you have to be at the stadium...?" she paused, "in two hours. And I suggest you get up before Duke thinks we spent the night

119

together."

Oh shit, you're right. However, not that I care what your brothers think you're mine Sassy, and I don't mind telling all of them that you belong to me. I just have to get through tomorrow's game first."

Zoey was quiet. Duke certainly was not going to be happy about that.

"Sassy what's wrong?" Yaz sounded concerned.

"Nothing, I just got a lot of work to do, call you later," she said before clicking off.

What's wrong with her, shouldn't you be happy he said that you are mine. Doesn't that mean something?

"Hey boss," Cara her assistant entered the office.

Zoey head rose. "Morning," she greeted.

"You okay boss?"

"I'm fine Cara, really just over thinking."

"If it's about that fine Yaz Bryant I'm all ears," she chuckled.

Zoey face heated. Did it show she slept with Yaz? "There's nothing to tell Cara."

"Are you sure," she asked grinning.

"Does it show?" Zoey said sheepishly.

Cara squealed clapping her hands. "Finally, I'm so proud of you. So how was it?" She gushed.

Zoey's head fell back against a chair. "It was all I thought it would be and then some, but...,"

"No, no, no. Zoey, don't start doubting what you feel. I think Yaz really likes you," she said with confidence.

Zoey looked doubtful anyway. "Please Cara no more, I need to think. I don't want to get hurt like before and we were not even intimate. I was a mess. If he decides he doesn't want me...," she paused, "and now that I know what it's like to be held and loved by him, I will not recover Cara, it will kill me because I love him so much."

"You're right, you are over thinking. Let things happen and stop looking for a reason why he will not want you. Okay."

"Okay," Zoey replied reluctantly.

You have an ice skater coming in around nine thirty," Cara informed.

"Pro?" Zoey groaned.

"And she thinks her stuff don't stink at," Cara commented before leaving the office.

Chapter 14

Jim met Calvin at ten in the parking garage where Zoey's office was located. For once Calvin did something right. At eight o'clock he called to say her car was still parked in her spot and she had not come out. Now at ten, she was still in the office.

Jim drove up and parked beside Calvin at the end of the partially deserted garage, Calvin lowered his window.

"Jim this ain't gonna work," Calvin complained. "Yaz ain't into her like that. He ain't gonna pay $50,000 for her."

"Oh, he'll pay, and so will those brothers of hers," Jim said smugly.

"You gonna get money from them too?" Calvin said frowning.

"Damn right, if they want the little bitch back they gotta pay, now keep your eyes open, when you see her step on your brakes. I'll know she's coming out."

Calvin frowned. "That's it? That's your weak ass plan?"

"How hard could it be to grab the bitch and throw her in the back your car?"

"And take her where Jim? I ain't doin this. I ain't doin no time in no Federal Prison for a botched up kidnapping scheme. Call the hotline, I don't give a damn. I didn't kill Aunt Martha. This is way out a hand and I ain't goin' to jail for you or my mother." Calvin peeled out of the parking garage.

"Stupid bastard," Jim cursed. Shit, he'll do it himself. He will get the bitch that ruined his life, and when her brothers and Yaz pay for her return, he'll kill her and leave the country. Jim remained silent watching, nearly salivating over the things he was going to do to the woman who ruined his life. He was glad he had the foresight to call in reinforcements. He had a feeling punk ass Calvin was going to back out.

Zoey stretched the muscles in her neck as she looked at the clock on the wall. It was ten thirty, and time to go home. At least, she was all caught up on all the patient files, and anyway, Duke said if she wasn't home in thirty minutes he was coming after her. That was five minutes ago.

Just as she put the last file away, her phone vibrated at her side. Probably Duke again.

Without looking at the screen or taking the phone from the holder on her side, she answered the auto speaker. "I'm coming!" She snapped.

"For whom Sassy!" Yaz voice yelled into the quiet room.

"Yaz?"

"For whom are you coming?" He snapped.

"Only for you Yaz," she purred.

"That's right."

"Aren't you supposed to be playing football?"

"It's halftime, I needed to hear your voice."

Zoey's heart swelled with happiness. "That's so sweet, and I miss you too."

"Are you home yet?"

"I'm on my way out now Yaz; I'll call you when I get home."

"You better," he threatened playfully.

"I will," she promised.

"Sassy?" He said the name so sultrily that it sent chills up her spine.

"Yes."

"I love you; call me as soon as you get home."

"Yaz! Yaz! What...?" Zoey snatched the phone from her hip and stared at it. The call ended and a slow grin began spreading on her face.

"I love you too," she whispered.

Zoey turned off the lights and set the alarm. It was always their habit when Zoey worked late; she would call Duke and have him on speaker as she drove home.

She pressed the number one and waited for Duke to answer. "Duke, I'm going to the garage now."

"Okay, Pud. Be careful I'm right here with you."

"Yaz called," she told him.

"Is he alright?" Duke asked concerned.

"Yes, he's fine. Duke, do you like Yaz?" She asked as she stepped off the elevator to the garage. "Damn, it's dark up here, "she commented looking around. "I need to call the city and let them know the lights are out."

"Hurry up and get in your car Zola," Duke said testily.

She didn't reply , she was too busy getting her keys from her bag.

"Zola!" Duke shouted.

"Okay, I'm hurrying."

"You didn't answer, girl you scared me."

"I'm going to the car now."

Zoey felt an eerie feeling creep up her spine as she walked quickly to her car and reached to pull open the door. Before getting in, she looked over her shoulder when a fist connected with her face. She fell hard against the car and was slightly dazed, unknowingly disconnecting the phone. The attacker wore a mask but he was definitely male and there was something familiar about him. It was his cologne, a scent she had smelled before and thought was a cheap scent at the time.

"Duke!" She shouted. There was no response.

"Come on bitch," the gravelly voice said snatching her away from the car. Zoey went into fight mode. She didn't have a black belt or anything, but she did take self-defense courses at the insistence of her brothers. When the assailant snatched her arm, Zoey took her heavy purse and swung connecting with her attacker's head. He snatched her purse and threw it to the ground. She turned to run hoping to put some distance from the attacker when another masked man stepped out of the darkness grabbing her rounded neck and slamming her to the concrete floor. Dazed, she lay still.

"Don't hurt her yet," the other man joined them gasping for breath.

Both men stood over her. "Where we gonna take her," the deeper voice culprit replied.

"Don't talk so much," the gravelly voiced one ordered, "you'll see."

Zoey lay still to ease her hand beneath her shirt to her phone. But the man bent over her before she could press the button.

"What do you want?" Zoey asked as the man snatched her to her feet.

"Shut up bitch," the raspy-voiced man growled.

Being her mouthy self, Zoey replied. "Damn where did you buy that cologne, from skunk's r us?"

"Shut up!" The leader yelled. "Still got that smart ass mouth I see, you won't be talking smart when I get done with you."

Although she was trembling inside, she didn't let them see her fear. "Call me a bitch again. Hey, you sound like somebody I know."

"Stop talkin so much," the deep voice warned the leader.

She didn't know who these morons were, but the scent of one was so familiar. "Wait are you kidnapping me?"

"Shut up!" The deep voice growled. "Knock her ass out, this bitch don't know when to shut up." Before the fist connected with her chin, Zoey knew who the leader is.

Zoey awakened to her face throbbing painfully. Her eyes darted around the room until they adjusted to the darkness. The place smelled musty and damp, she surmised that she must be in a basement or cellar. The only light she saw through her swollen blurred eyes was coming from the door at the top of the stairs. A rag as tied around her mouth, and he began to struggle against her restraints that had her hands and legs bound. In the distance, she heard loud muffled voices but could not make out the words. Zoey wiggled her wrists around hoping to loosen the bonds or, at least, stretch them enough to wiggle her small hands free. She worked diligently trying to free herself while tears of frustration slipping down her face. Feeling the ties loosen slightly, and with the fingers of one hand, she gripped the rope. She had to, at least, get one of her hands free and the only way she could do that was to pull her hand out. She gritted her teeth to do what she had to do to get free. With clenched teeth to keep from crying out and pulled her hand from the small opening. She felt her skin slide off as she painfully freed her hand cringing as she felt the blood from the wound drip to her palm. Instantly she felt for the phone that was attached to her waist and sighed relieved when she found it was still there, thankful those two moron's didn't check her or they would have found the phone clipped to her waist. She couldn't see anything except a sliver of light coming from beneath the door and the glow from the phone through the narrow slits of her eyes.

She snatched the rag from her mouth, lifted the phone and saw that she lost connection and had only two bars. She had to do something fast. With a GPA on her phone, she could send a signal where she was to Duke. She pressed the speed dial number for Duke.

"Zoey! My god baby..."

"Duke," she whispered. "It was Jim who took me."

"Are you hurt?" Duke asked frantically. She could hear her brothers in the background.

"I think I'm in the basement somewhere. He has this other guy with him, but I don't think it's Calvin," she said continued whispering.

Zoey I called the police; try to keep your phone open and we will find you."

"Hurry Duke, I don't have much power. Duke, they're coming! I'm scared!"

"Be brave Pud, you're a Howard."

"Just hurry Duke!"

Jim and Dex stood up in Margaret's kitchen as Jim paced the floor, profusely sweating. He had to figure out what to do with his prisoner's body when he killed her. He knew he had the move from where he is because this place was too open, too obvious. He tried to call Calvin, but he would not pick up. Cursing, he stuck to phone in his pocket

"When I see that Calvin I'm gonna hurt him real bad," Jim threatened.

"I don't give a shit what you do with Calvin, give me my money so I can go, you on your own playa. I helped you get the bitch; I'm gone."

Jim glared at Dex. "I still need you. You gotta help me find another spot, this place is to open."

"Man, you're only givin' me $500, you now talkin' bout killing the girl. I want no part that, just give me my money so I can go."

"I will pay you well Dex, just stick it out, I promise there is enough for both of us."

"I don't know, man. This plan a yours is shaky. I ain't gonna down with you Jim, so give me my money so I can go man."

Jim scrubbed his hand down his face exasperated. "Shit, give me a minute to get it together."

"You think she woke up yet?" Dex asked.

"She'll wake up after I slap the taste out of her mouth," Jim said through tight lips.

"What she do that got you hating her so bad?"

"She messed with my money," Jim answered. "Nobody messes with my money."

"How? She stole it?"

"No, that bitch turn Yaz against me. Showed him how I was cheating him, that's what she did."

"You was ripping off Yaz Bryant?" Dex asked shocked. "I thought he was your boy?"

"Shut up Dex, I gave him my life. If it weren't for me his ass would have been in jail or working in some factory..., Jim paused.

"What's that? You hear that?"

"What? I don't hear nothing."

"Shut up!" Jim went to the window and lifted a blind peering out. He didn't see anything so he turned back to Dex.

"Come on let's get this bitch up," Jim ordered.

Zoey heard them move to the door, she quickly covered her mouth with the rag and dropped her head like she was still unconscious. The two men came down the steps and stood in front of her.

Jim turned to the door listening. "I think someone's outside," Jim said looking up at the door.

"Come on man you just paranoid let's move this bitch and go."

"Come on somebody is outside," Jim said moving up the steps with Dex following behind.

Zoey heard it too, hoping it was the police. Her head rose from loud voices and banging heard overhead. She snatched the rag from her mouth.

"Zola! Zola!" Duke shouted.

"Down here Duke!" She shouted.

Duke's large body barreled down the steps with a police officer following closely behind him. Someone switched on the light momentarily blinding her. Duke found her sitting in a chair with her legs tied and a rag around her neck. He stooped down in front of her.

"Baby, are you alright! He asked his tone choked.

"Not as bad as Jim wanted me to be," she joked, as tears flowing down her swollen face.

Duke quickly untied her ankles lifting her in his arms and carrying her up the stairs and out of the house.

Zoey pressed her face into Duke's neck. Satch, Jelly, Cab, and Dizzy circled them. Zoey's arms tightened around his neck.

"Come on baby looked at us," Cab coaxed gently rubbing her back.

It was just about dawn, and the rising of this sun was highlighting the sky.

"Come on baby look at us," Satch gently coaxed.

Zoey raised her head. Her eyes were swollen practically shut, dried blood was under her nose and the corner of her mouth split.

"Hell no! Where is that bastard," Dizzy yelled, followed by cursing from her other three brothers. Duke was unnaturally quiet, which was not good.

"I am taking our baby home," he stated calmly moving away from his brothers. After he had settled Zoey in the car, he turned to his brothers.

I am not bailing your asses out of jail and I don't visit jailbirds." He got into the driver's seat of his car and waited. After much grumbling, his brother's joined him, and silently they drove home.

Chapter 15

At duke's insistent Zoey stayed in his part of the mansion, as well as the four brothers who refuse to leave her. She had not spoken since she had arrived, all five brothers doted and coddled the unresponsive Zoey.

After a much needed shower, and all her wounds were cleaned and dressed, Duke put her to bed with a hot cup of spiked tea so she can rest. He told the police they could get a statement after his sister was taking care of.

Ensured that Zoey was sleeping the brothers convened into the fitness room to discuss what happened and blow off some steam. When Duke entered the gym, each brother was focused on venting. Satch was on a treadmill running inclined at top speed. Cab was beating the crap out of the body bag, and Jelly left training camp when he was informed of Zoey missing and was on the bike pedaling like he was a cyclist in the Tour De France and Diz was beating the hell out of the punching bag. Duke knew he also needed to let off some steam but opted to wait until later. Now he needed his family and his family needed their older level-headed brother.

The brothers noticed him standing quietly in the doorway and stopped. Tears flowed unchecked from his eyes, tears he didn't care who saw. That bastard tried to hurt their baby, the heart of this family of men. Life would have been over for them if they lost Zoey and the thought would have killed them all. When Duke looked at his brothers with tears falling unashamed down his face, they went to him and embraced their elder brother.

"She's home Duke and she's safe," Dizzy's said as his arms closed around his brother, and the five of them embraced each other letting tears of rage seep from their souls, for if they did not Jim and his accomplice would never see the inside of a courtroom.

When the tears slowly subsided and some semblances of the brothers was restored Duke spoke first. "Come on, let's eat," Duke invited.

"Not if you are cooking," Jelly grimaced.

Cab chortled. Satch patted the glaring Duke on the back.

"I'm ordering Chinese," he replied indignantly as he moved passed his grinning brothers. Dizzy shook his head following Satch.

She screamed as she felt her skin being scrapped from her arms as she was drawn across the concrete floor.

"When I'm finished with you bitch, you're dead," the menacing voice shouted before throwing her in the pitch black car.

Her attacker snatched off his mask and Yaz's face loomed before her, his gray eyes pitch black with hate.

"Why Yaz? I love you," she cried.

His head fell back and he laughed loudly. "You ruined my friendship," he chanted.

"No, no! Yaz no, I love you...," She screamed.

Zoey! Zoey Baby," Duke called as she tossed and turned.

"Pick her up," Satch cried.

Duke lifted her on his lap cradling her like a small child. Finally, her eyes open, meeting the worried gaze of each brother.

"Zo?" Jelly call softly.

Tears fell as she saw the sadness in their eyes.

"I'm sorry," she muttered, "I'm sorry."

"Pud, sorry for what, you did nothing," Duke replied holding her close.

128

Zoey laid her head on his chest, glad her brothers were with her, she just hated seeing the sadness in their eyes the because of her.

"Are you hungry Pud? Got your favorite," Duke replied with a weak smile.

Zoey shook her head. "No, I just want to lie down, please."

Duke lay her down tucking the covers around her. After each brother had kissed her forehead, they all filed out, the last one out turning off the light.

Zoey screamed. "No! Turn it back on!"

"Okay, baby okay."

Zoey rolled over giving them her back. "Don't turn off the light," she softly.

Duke stood for a minute watching her. This has affected her deeper than all of them realized.

The brothers later sat quietly each with their own thoughts.

"These are the times I miss our parents," Jelly thought out loud.

"Maybe she needs to see a doctor," Satch replied and started pacing the floor.

"I know what she needs," Duke said coming to his feet leaving the room. The brother's looked at each other confused.

Duke ease into Zoey's room and search for her phone, finding it lying on the bureau. He looked back at his baby sister curled up in a fetal position. For all of Zoey's sauciness she was devastated by the attack, and although it has only been a few hours, he didn't want her wallowing in this. She was strong and she had to bounce back. He moved close to the bed and kissed her gently on her bruised cheek before leaving the room.

A rage he never knew grabbed him and Jim Bailey and his partner should be thankful the police got to them first. He had no doubt he would have killed the son of a bitch without a second thought. Duke left the room door ajar so he could hear if Zoey had another nightmare.

As he moved through the house, he played all the events of the night. It was always a rule if she worked late to put him or any of the other brothers on speaker so they knew she made it safely to her car. When he heard her shout his name, his heart drop and then the phone went dead. He called back but only her voice mail picked up. After several tries, he started to panic and called his brothers. The only one he could not reach was Jelly, who was in training camp, but he left the message. By the time they all arrived at the parking garage,

129

Zoey was gone and her purse was thrown on the floor of the garage, and her car was still pasrked, but nothing was missing. That told Duke it was not a robbery. Panic began to set in all the brothers. Duke called Charles Hayden, a former FBI agent and a good friend with his own Security and Investigation Company, the best in the city. Charles wasted no time coming. After three in the morning, his phone rang. It was Zoey and she was whispering. She said she was in a basement somewhere. He instructed her to keep her phone on and in less than thirty minutes, Charles tech team knew where she was being held. The police were notified, and after explaining the situation, the brothers were in his Hummer and driving to Mount Airy. The house they discover was owned by Yaz's Aunt Margaret. Duke and his brothers wanted to barrel into the house, but the police that surrounded the house made them remain back. As the SWAT team silently surrounded, each brother praying no gunfire was necessary.

Like the idiot he is, Jim Bailey opened the door and was met with fifteen armed police guns drawn. All he could do was surrender. He then rushed into the house and down to the basement where he found his baby trembling as tears coursed down her swollen, beaten face. He had to hold himself in check when all he wanted to do was get his baby out of that house. When he lifted her in his arms, she curled her small body tightly against his chest as if her life depended on it. When he got her home, he remained calm as he tended to her injuries. Her eyes were swollen shut, her lip was split at the corner and he thought her nose was broken because of the dried blood, but thankful it was not. The whole time he tended to her, she had not responded and this worried him. The only time he was sure she was lucid is when he'd cleaned and dressed and wounds around her wrist where the skin was rubbed off where she had pulled her hand free from the ropes that bounded her. Zoey hadn't spoken since they took her home only when she had a nightmare and to tell them to keep the light on.

Duke sat in his study, it was 3:00 am Wednesday morning. Neither brother has slept since Zoey came home. He realized that he needed help with her and the five men were not going to be able to do it. Dealing with his brother's simmering rage was not something he wanted to do. He thought about calling Yaz but decided to wait until he returned from Atlanta later in the day. This will be a test of his feelings for his baby sister, when he finally found out about the extent of his ex-managers greed and about how he attempted to

130

hurt Zoey.

Duke scrolled down her contact list. Caitlin Smith. He hadn't spoken to her since she fled Hershey Park upset with him for what, he didn't know. His early doubts about her had faded long ago. It was true, they knew nothing about her past only that she was Zoey's best friend, and the one thing he can say for sure is that Caitlin loved Zoey and Zoey loved Caitlin. At this point it didn't matter how he felt about her, Zoey needed her now. He knew he should wait until after dawn and call but he could not, because right now Zoey needed her friend.

Caitlin was jarred awake by the ringing of her home phone. She squinted at the bedside clock. "Three in the morning, who in the hell is calling me at this ungodly hour," she grumbled. She looked at the caller ID. "Zoey," she whispered. She answering the phone quickly. "Zoey what wrong?" She sounded frantic.

"Caitlin," a deep voice replied.

"Who are you and what are you doing with Zoey's phone?" She shouted into the phone.

"Caitlin, it's Duke!" He said into the phone.

"Ellington, what's wrong, where Zoey?"

"I need you," Duke said his voice strained.

"I'll be right there," Caitlin replied without thought.

"My plane will be there by 7 am, I will have a limo pick you up at home; I need an address."

Normally Caitlin would have argued. If Ellington was sending his private plane from Philly to New York, this was not good. She gave him her address assuring she'll be ready. "Is she OK?"

"No...," he paused. "How long can you...,"

"As long as it takes," she interrupted.

Yaz couldn't wait to get back to his Zoey. Damn he missed her. He tried to call her after the game several times only to have her voice mail pick up. He was feeling especially good today. He had a good game and was sure if the team held up they would make the playoffs. Since it was a late game Monday, the team stayed unti Tuesday to rest up and would arrive in Philadelphia Wednesday mid-morning. He knew the airport in Philly would be full of reporters and this was one time he was glad one of the Howard brothers were coming to intervene for him. His only thoughts were about seeing his Sassy. Which was strange? Before he left, Satch left a message Monday afternoon saying something came up and they would not make the game, he would be at the airport to pick him up.

When the plane landed Yaz's heart escalated, soon he would see his Sassy.

As he expected, reporters were crowded at the gate. Yaz looked around for Satch, who was supposed to pick him up.

"Mr. Bryant, great game," a reported commented catching his attention.

"Thanks," he responded still looking out for Satch.

"Mr. Bryant, what are your thoughts on your former Manager Jim Bailey being arrested for kidnapping and the attempted murder of Dr. Zola Howard?"

"What?"

"Is it true that you fired him for embezzlement?"

Blood drain from Yaz's face, and he felt faint. Zoey murdered? Where was Satch?

"It is alleged that your mother accepted bribes from rogue scouts, during your college days, is that true?"

The reporters crowding around him suddenly became a silent, all wanting to hear his response. Yaz focused on the reporter who asked a question.

"What the fuck did you say?" He asked his heart pounding in his chest. Just when Yaz drew back his fist, Satch grabbed him from behind. Yaz turned to glare at the person who dared to interfere.

"Yaz stop!" Satch calmly said.

His head was pounding as rapidly as his heart while the reporters sent a barrage of questions and speculations at him. Satch spoke loudly over at the crowd surrounding them and announced, "At 5:00 PM a press conference will be held at the Howard Building conference room, that's all."

"Come on Yaz," Satch ordered as they push through the reporters to the waiting limo outside the gate.

Yaz sat silently in the limo, trying desperately to absorb what he just heard. Satch got into the limo sitting across from him. Tears wavered in Yaz's eyes. "What the hell is going on? What happened to Zoey?" He asked choking on his words.

"Jim Bailey kidnapped her with the intent to ransom her to you and to us."

"What?" Did he...?"

"We found them in time. He did beat her, but she's OK. Jim and his accomplice were caught."

"Calvin?"

"No, some dude named Dex. Calvin was not involved in this, but he knows something. It seems that Calvin and your Aunt Margaret left Philly."

Yaz head fell back against the seat. "I need to see Zoey."

"You will, we're hoping you can get her to respond."

"What do you mean?"

"She hasn't spoken since we found her two days ago."

Yaz started to tremble and the tears he held in check ran down his face unabashed. "My God," Yaz moaned and sobbed into his hands.

"That's right, get it out now," Satch encouraged. "because right now we need you to be strong when you see her."

Caitlin arrived and looked up at Duke taking note of the sadness and worry in his bronze eyes. He moved aside letting her past.

"Thank you, Caitlin, I don't know...,"

Cat walked up and gently cupped his face. "She's my friend, no need to thank me."

She turned and went into the parlor. She really loved how he had the room decorated, with its neutral colors and comfortable furnishings. There were many things about Ellington's house she loved. She sat in the Queen Anne chair while Duke sat on the sofa across from her. "What happened Ellington?" Caitlin asked.

Not wanting to go into detail, Duke told her about the kidnapping and attempt on Zoey's life. He explained they were not clear why Yaz's ex-manager did this.

"Does Yaz know what has happened?" Caitlin inquired.

"Satch went to get him from the airport and we are hoping he doesn't know anything until he gets here."

"The boys? Caitlin asked.

"Finally went to bed and should soon be up. They stayed since Zoey...," Duke stood up quickly moving away.

"Ellington everything is going to be fine," she says soothingly. "I promise."

"She hasn't spoken since we got her back.," he said with his back still to her.

Cat rose and stood behind him, badly wanting to comfort him and make him feel better.

"Hey Cat," Jelly greeted, followed Cab and Dizzy.

"Good morning, I'm so sorry about Zoey."

"The brothers each expressed their joy at seeing her as much as they could considering the situation. Cat smiled. She genuinely liked Zoey's brothers minus Ellington. The jury was still out on him.

"After I see about Zoey I'll make a nice breakfast."

"No," Duke said finally turning and Cat did not miss the moisture in his eyes. "That's not...,"

"Ellington, I don't mind and I know you guy's probably haven't eaten well in couple days."

"Caitlin...,"

"Ellington," she interrupted, "take me to see Zoey, and then I'll fix breakfast, really I don't mind," she replied glaring at him.

The doorbell rang. "Who the hell is at 8:00 in the morning?" Duke roared.

"I'll get it," Cab offered.

Cat and Duke stood close, but not touching.

"Oh, Duke honey why didn't you call me?" Victoria Thomas cried as she sailed into the room pushing between Cat and Duke throwing herself into Duke's arms. He had no choice, but to catch her. Cat's eyes widened as they met the stunned Ellington's eyes.

"Victoria, what are you doing here?"

"Darling, I came to help."

Victoria was dressed immaculately in her Donna Karen pantsuit, Vera Cruz pumps, and expensively weaved hair hanging past her shoulders in loose curls framing her fair overdone makeup face for someone to have just rushed over here at eight o'clock in the morning. She looked over at Caitlin with narrow eyes.

"Victoria it was not necessary for you to come over here," Duke said moving away from her him and stood beside Caitlin.

"Duke of course it is, I like Zola and maybe one day we will be sisters."

Caitlin exhaled. "Can someone show me where Zoey's room is, please," she said turning away.

"I will show you," Cab offered smirking at Duke. Duke's eyes narrowed at his brother.

"Who's that Duke? If you needed a housekeeper, I could have helped you with that. She doesn't look like she could keep a house," Victoria whispered loudly.

Cat stopped to confront the fake witch, but Cab pulled her along.

"Victoria, go home!" Duke replied and followed Cab and Cat.

Victoria looked at Jelly and Dizzy grinning at her like idiots.

"No, he didn't!" She hissed as her face turned two shades pink. She turned to follow Duke, but Jelly and Dizzy grabbed her by the arms and showed her to the door.

"Goodbye Vicki," they said gently pushing her out the door. The last thing that needed now was that drama queen upsetting their sister.

Duke, Cab, and Caitlin stood outside the door.

"I want to see her alone," she told them as she reached to open the door.

Slowly Cat pushed the door open and glanced at her and gasped inwardly at the damage to her face. Zoey lay on her back awake staring listlessly at the ceiling. Cat went to her and slipped into the bed and lay beside her on the large sleigh bed and looked at the ceiling with her. At a closer examination, thankfully her wounds were all superficial and would heal, leaving no scars on her beautiful face.

"Hey Chick," Caitlin greeted as they always did since college.

No response.

"Zoey don't you dare let this break you. I won't let you wallow in this for three reasons. First, because I love you very much, you're all I have. Second, both of us can't be mental. And, third, you have five brothers and a boyfriend who loves you very much. So Chick we are going to get over this, and after you're feeling better, we are going to go down to that jail and kicked Jim Bailey's natural black ass." Still Zoey didn't respond.

"Look at me Zoey, let me know you are listening to me."

Still no reply from her girl and it bothered her. Zoey rolled away from Cat.

"Oh no, you don't Chick!" Cat shouted sitting up in the bed. "Don't you ignore me! Didn't I teach you all you have is your self-respect, pride and a great right hook baby? So, Zola Ella Howard don't you dare shut me out." Cat rose from the bed.

"Now I'm going out there to fix some breakfast for those malnutrition brothers of yours. Oh, guess who I just met? Your future sister-in-law," Cat replied with a chuckle. "I can just see you and Victoria la-de-daing at the country club, eating watercress sandwiches and drinking tea with your pinky extended. She's right outside, I can send her in so you can bond." Cat chuckled.

"Oh no you don't Chick," Zoey grumbled through her swollen lips.

Cat grinned. "That's my girl."

"Cat," she mumbled. Cat got back on the bed and Zoey fell into her arms sobbing.

Moments later while the two lay a holding each other, Zoey spoke. "I look like crap, right?"

Cat leaned up and studied her face. "You wanted the truth or the lie?"

"The lie of course."

"Girl you are fine, more beautiful than the first Miss Black America," she replied straight face. And Zoey smiled and then groaned.

"I'm sorry Chick. No more laughing until you lose those botox lips. Are you hungry? Zoey nodded.

"OK, let's see what we can get past those soup coolers." Cat rose from the bed and Zoey groaned and covered her mouth to keep from laughing.

"Okay, let me go feed New Jersey's five starved refugees, and I'll come back and you can take a long hot bath, and afterward I'll give you a pedicure, does wonders for...," she paused, "well does wonders."

"See ya Chick," Zoey mumbled through clenched teeth.

"See ya Chick." Cat blew her a kiss.

"I want to see my brothers," she stated.

OK if you really want to." Zoey nodded. When Cat had left and close the door behind her, she exhaled as the tears welled in her eyes. She found the brothers waiting for word from her.

"Where's your sister-in-law?" She asked the brothers ignoring Ellington.

"We put her out," Jelly stated. "Duke wouldn't."

"Caitlin, how is Zoey?" Duke asked his tone concerned.

"For some reason she wants to see her brothers," she stated.

"Really?" Cab shouted exuberantly. Everyone came to their feet quickly and she was surrounded by three overly tall men throwing a barrage of questions at her. Duke stood back smiling. "What did she say? Is she in pain?"

"Hush fools!" Caitlin shouted. "She wants to see her brothers, and no not too much. Now, refugees, I'm going to fix breakfast while you visit with your sister."

Cat watched as they rushed to see their sister and Duke remained behind and when he got close to Caitlin he stopped.

"Caitlin, thank you," Duke said.

"I love her too," She said sincerely looking up at him. Duke reached out to touch her face, but Cat turned away. "I'm going to make breakfast," she announced.

Duke watched as Cat hurried away from him wondering if she was only skittish around him or all men. There was something about Caitlin that intrigued him, and not just her beauty or commanding presence, but something that went deeper and feeling the need to protect her was overwhelming. There was also that ceded sadness in her eyes that she tried to mask with flippant talk and remarks, but he saw through it. Right now he had to focus on Zoey, and then after all this drama is done, his main objective will be Caitlin Smith.

Chapter 16

Zoey sat propped against the pillows listening to her brothers and their light banter back and forth. The only one not present was Duke.

"You're sure you are alright, Little Bit?" Jelly asked. He was the closest to her in the age, being only five years older. Duke has been head of the family since she was five years old, and was more of a father figure to her in a lot of ways. He even spanked her once when she played hooky from school when she was 12 years old. Zoey smiled at the memory.

What, little bit?" Cab asked.

Zoey shook her head. "I just remembered when Duke had to spank me." They remembered as well because brothers chuckled.

"You were running through the house like the devil himself with after you," Cab added.

"He was," Zoey mumbled chuckling.

"You know, Duke regrets that still to this day," Dizzy's replied.

"Yeah, but I learned my lesson. It hurts me more to see Duke's disappointment in me. I vowed never to do anything that would make him feel like that again I never want to disappoint any of you.

"You could never disappoint us Zoey," Dizzy said taking her hand.

"We love you Pud, you are our baby," Duke said leaning against a door frame.

"I know."

"Caitlin's making breakfast," Duke informed them. They didn't move, each reluctant to leave their little sister's side.

"You had better go, Cat's claws show when she cooks for nothing," Zoe warned playfully.

When the others were gone, Duke sat beside her on the bed. Zoey moved closer and lay her head on his shoulder.

"Zoey, Satch has gone to pick up Yaz from the airport and is bringing him here," he told her wanting to see how she reacted to the news.

Zoey lifted her head. "I don't want to see him," Zoey replied.

"Why Baby?"

"I don't want him to see me like this," Zoey admitted.

"We're hoping he doesn't know anything until we tell him before the papers came out. It's possible the news of what happened has already been on the TV stations." Duke paused. "Zoey you need to know when he finds out he will want to see you."

Duke was right. Right now they've needed each other. Jim was responsible for his mother's death and almost hers and the guilt is going to overwhelm him. Zoey knew she had to be there for Yaz because she loved him.

Satch and Yaz sat outside in the limo.

"I want to see Zoey first, and then I want to see Jim," Yaz requested. "I need to know why," he said shaking his head confused.

"Okay Yaz let's go," Satch said getting out of the limo.

Yaz felt like he was mourning his mother all over again, knowing that Jim had something to with his mother's death, pondering if Calvin and his mother had anything to do with it? If they knew about this all these years and didn't come forward with what they knew, he would not rest until they were all rotting in prison.

Yaz followed Satch inside and Duke was the first greet him, echoed by his brothers. Satch immediately filled them in on what happened at the airport and the press conference he planned for later in the day.

"How is Zoey?" Yaz asked.

"She'll be alright," Duke answered.

"Did Jim hurt her badly?"

"She's bruised and swollen, but she'll be okay. Do you want to see her?" Yaz shook his head.

Yaz felt responsible for Zoey's assault. He thought he could see her, but his guilt made him not able to face her.

"Yaz, I don't think that's a good idea," Duke informed him.

"He's right," Zoey said behind him as she entered the den where they all stood.

Yaz turned and pain he has never felt before sliced through him. The sight of her face all bruised and battered caused deep hurt in his soul. His eyes hardened and the guilt and rage he tried so hard to quell came to the surface. It was a good thing Jim was incarcerated, for he would hunt him down and would have gladly killed him. Yaz turned away sharply.

"Don't you do it, Yazair Bryant," Zoey snapped taking in the guilt and anger she saw in his eyes.

His terse body had tightened before he turned to face her, but Zoey had moved closer to him. "Don't you dare shut me out," her eyes glaring into his defiantly.

Yaz met her gaze and was lost in the umber eyes as tear filled eyes. Yaz reached his large hand out to her and Zoey could see the slight tremble. She placed her hand in his and he gently pulled her closer. He lifted her chin and studied her bruised face and for every scratch and bruised she had his blood boil to almost overflowing. Zoey felt the tension in his body.

"Yaz," she whispered. His thumb softly caressed her lower lip as he studied her face while hot tears welled and spilled over rolling down his handsome face. It hurt him deeply knowing the pain she endured because of Jim's greed and him not being here to protect her.

She wrapped her arms around him placing her face in his chest and sobbed. Unmindful of the audience, Yaz lifted Zoey into his arms as he carried her to the room.

Caitlin stood in the doorway and watched the exchange, wishing she could love the way those two young people obviously loved one another. Her eyes met Duke's after brief pause Caitlin turned and walked away.

Yaz lay Zoey gently on the bed and lay down beside her. Both were quiet as they stared at the ceiling.

"Yaz... Zoey," they spoke at the same time and then turn to face each other. She pressed her hand to his chest Yaz pressed a finger to her lips. "Let me go first," he whispered.

"Baby, I'm sorry this happened. I should have...,"

Zoey shook her head. "No Yaz."

"Shh…, I should have never involved you in my drama."

"How could you not know Jim was insane?"

Yaz chuckled and then sobered quickly. "He hurt you, baby, I can't have any man putting their hands on you," he growled. "I would not hesitate to kill any man that did. Did you know he may be responsible for my mother's death?"

"I did after he kidnapped me. I'm so sorry Yaz."

"I've mourned her a long time, the only thing I can say is I now have closure knowing who was may be responsible. I'm sorry he did this to you, but I need you to understand something.

"What?" Zoey said not sure if she was going to like what he was about to say.

Yaz took her hands lifting them to his lips. "I have so much anger and rage inside me baby and I need to be alone."

"No, Yaz no; don't do this, don't shut me out," she said alarmed pulling her hands from his.

"Listen! Listen to me!" Yaz stressed.

Zoey looked into his smoky eyes. She could see the pain and anger deep inside them.

"Zoey I don't want to hurt you but now I need to do some soul searching. I'm going to take time away football, first...," Zoey gasped.

Tears rolled down her bruised face and Yaz gently wiped them away. "Give me this Zoey, please."

"I c-can't," she hiccupped. "When Jim had me tied up that basement, the only thing I thought about was getting out and coming to you Yaz. I need you. She paused as her heart pounded. "I love you so much, it hurts when I don't see or know where you are. I want you to make love to me as you did before all this happened for the rest of my life. I do understand what you're saying and as selfish and pathetic as this sounds I won't let you shut me out. Not a Trish, Jim, Calvin or my brothers as much as I love them will stop me from being with you."

Yaz's heart swelled with love for her and all he can think is, MINE.

"Please, Yaz together we can get through this. Unless you don't...,"

Yaz's mouth covered hers. Zoey winced but did not stop him. Her arms went around him holding him tightly to her. Yaz rolled her to her back and settled between her legs. His manhood throbbed against her center and Zoey lifted her hips against him wanting him inside her. Yaz rolled from her and quickly came to his feet.

"Yaz?" Zoey called afraid that he was leaving. She could not bear that. When she pathetically bared her soul to him, he never responded. Maybe he didn't love her, and maybe he was going to take his pain and anger and leave her. He lifted his shirt over his head, towed off his Italian loafers dropping his pants and underwear in one move. Zoey exhaled a nervous breath when Yaz knelt beside her and slowly undressed her until she was nude. His fingers caressed her already sensitive nipples before taking it into his mouth. Zoey arched off the bed holding his head lovingly as he feasted on her breasts. His lips trailed slowly over her skin tasting her he before traveled down to her tight stomach with fiery wet kisses. He needed to taste her, he needed to recall her flavor and sweet fragrance. Zoey moaned and withered beneath his questing mouth. Yaz grasped her hips to still them and wasted no time feed from her sweet nectar. He wanted to drive her crazy with her need for him before he filled her with his thick throbbing member. He loved Zoey's responsive, passionate nature and it turned him on making him want to take her fast and hard. Yet, he had to refrain. This was only the second time they made love and he had to ease her into his dominant sexual ways.

Yaz please, I can't take it," she said breathlessly.

Yaz lifted his head. "Yes, baby you can. Don't you come yet, hold on for me."

He knew Zoey wanted to move but Yaz clasped tightly in his grip. Her first lesson was obedience, and he has her almost where he wanted her. Zoey's hand started grabbing for him as her thighs began to tremble. Now it was time to take what's his and in one swift move, Yaz was sliding inside her wet cavern and Zoey screamed as her orgasm took her over the edge. Yaz covered her mouth with his as he moved inside her almost losing control when her walls clamped tightly around him. He never felt anything like this and the way she loved him only enhance the feeling. Changing the pace of their lovemaking, Yaz needed her to come for him again. Yaz pulled out flipping her to her stomach. Zoey groaned missing the fullness of him inside her. Yaz leaned over her and whispered. "Get on your knees sweetheart." Zoey looked over her shoulder not understanding but complied. He pulled her body into his as his hot kisses trailed from her neck to her back. Zoey moaned gyrating her bottom into him.

"You have to be quiet," he chuckled. "I don't want your brothers to kill me." He grabbed her waist, she grabbed the headboard.
Arching her back offering herself to him and he entered slowly methodically moving in and out. He wanted her to beg for what she wanted and it wasn't long before she was pleading for him to take her faster.

"What baby, tell me what you want?" He crooned.

"Harder, Yaz harder," she moaned. He gifted her with her desire and moved harder, faster and it wasn't long before Zoey's walls tightened around him screaming her release. His legs started trembling as his hips piston inside her and then froze as her tight body milked him while she rode his throbbing manhood. His teeth sank into her shoulder to keep from shouting as she pulled his strength from him. His orgasm was hard and long. What has this woman done to him, because he never felt anything like it. Zoey's trembling body and she collapsed beneath him, with him on top of her. Yaz rolled to her side waiting for his heart to regulate and his body to stop trembling. He turned his head and their eyes met and the look in her eyes floored him. This beautiful woman loved him, he had no doubt. He never saw that in any other women he had been with in his past.

"Please, Yaz don't shut me out. I know you're angry inside, only together can we work it out. I love you."

Yaz pulled her close to him kissing her tenderly. "Together Sassy," he replied because he realized that there was no way he could be without her for a single minute. "Sassy know this is what you want because I'm not letting you go."

Zoey rolled on top of him grinning. "And I'm not going anywhere," she vowed.

Yaz felt himself getting hard. "Oh know you don't," he said rolling her off. As bad as he wanted to sink into her glorious body he wouldn't. It's bad enough the Howard brothers were going to kick his butt.

A knock sounded at the door and Yaz and Zoey looked at each other and grimaced. Yaz rose and slipped on his pants before going to the door. Outside to the door sat his bag. Grabbing the bag, he closed the door just as the intercom came on. It was Duke.

"Yaz there's a press conference at the office. We need him calm Pud."

"I want to go," Zoey said into the intercom.

"No!" Yaz and Duke said together.

"Why not this involves me too," she stated tersely.

"Talk to her Yaz. Meet us in the den at four.

Duke turned to Caitlin, who stood behind him. "They love each other," she said smiling.

"He made her scream," he countered frowning.

When they heard the first high-pitched sound coming from the back of the house, Cat had to threaten them with a weapon to keep the brothers from racing to Zoey's room. Cat sucked her teeth with her hands on her hips. "If you five don't know the difference between a distressed scream and a passionate scream you've got work to do Mr. Players from the Himalayas," she teased leaving a stunned the Duke.

"I bet I could make you scream," Duke boasted. Cat stopped in her tracks and turned.

"That will never happen," she replied as she turned the corner.

Duke smiled. "Oh, Caitlin Smith it will happen, maybe not now, but soon," he chuckled to himself.

Thanks to Satch's charm and Yaz's popularity the story of the Yaz Bryant and his ex-manager's attempted murder and kidnapping did not make front-page news. Oh, it was big, just Satch charmed the press into downplaying the story and it also helped that the Howard's were friends with the owner of the Inquirer. The only drama that came about was when an overzealous reporter commented about Yaz's mother and her involvement in the bribery scandal, and it took the five brothers to hold the big man back.

They now all sat at the table eating a late dinner Caitlin and Zoey prepared and everyone was unusually quiet.

"What's your intentions Yaz?" Duke asked gruffly breaking the silence. Zoey and Yaz head snapped up together their eyes met. Caitlin gasped.

"Intentions?" Yaz repeated swallowing hard.

"Yes damn it, intentions."

"Duke please!" Zoey cried.

"No, he is right," Cab agreed turning to glare at Yaz.

Caitlin looked at each one of Zoey's brothers and could not believe these uncouth Neanderthals. She lifted a roll and threw it beaning Duke right on his forehead. All eyes at the widened and mouths dropped open.

"Ellington, I need to see you in the kitchen," Cat demanded rising from the chair. Duke didn't rise; he just stared at her as if she had lost her mind. "Did you just hit me with bread?" He roared rising.   ·

"Now Ellington!" She ordered going into the kitchen. The others watched the exchange with great interest. Duke stomped after her.

"Now Yaz answered the damn question," Cab grumbled.

His reply was halted, when loud voices and noise could be heard from behind the kitchen door.

"You seem to forget Zoey is a grown woman. How could you?"

"What Caitlin? Of course, I want to know what his intentions are. She's my sister I will not see her hurt."

"Are you blind? You see how Yaz is with Zoey, they love each other.

"Tell me, how would you know what love is when you can't even stand to be touched!" he shouted back at her.

Caitlin's eyes narrowed at him. "Maybe so, but I know love when I see it!" she shouted back.

By now they were squared off and Duke's height hovering over her and she wasn't backing down. God, Duke wanted to kiss her. "To hell with that!" He pulled that into his arms and covered her mouth with his. Cat stiffened and then her arms circled his neck and

144

her mouth tasted exquisite. Duke feasted on her mouth and she opened up allowing it. Dukes arms tightened around her, and the kiss intensified and Caitlin purred. Duke lifted his head gazing at her upturned face and closed eyes.

"Caitlin," he whispered.

Her eyes snapped open. "Oh my God," she cried backing away. Fear was in her eyes like he never saw before. She did not black-out, she remembered it all. Ellington was kissing her and she didn't black out.

"Caitlin," Duke called reaching for her.

"No don't touch me," she cried frantically. Her eyes darted around. Why didn't I black out? She stilled. She knew why. It was not violent.

"He's the only one who..., I have to go," tears flowing from her eyes.

"Caitlin what happened?" Duke called as she ran from the kitchen opposite the dining room.

"What just happen?" He muttered scratching his head.

Duke returned to sit with his family. "Where's Cat?" Zoey asked. "Did you say some the hurt her feelings, Duke?"

Duke's eyes focused on his sister. He sprang from his chair taking the stairs two at a time. "Not, this time, Caitlin; you're not running out on me this time," he mumbled.

Cat opened the door with suitcase in hand. Duke blocked her. "Caitlin, why are you running?"

Cat put down the suitcase, stepping close to Duke and wrapped her arms around his waist her head resting his chest. She stepped back to look at him.

"Ellington, I have to go. I'm not well, but you showed me there's hope for me. Thank you."

Caitlin talk to me, tell me what's wrong." She reached up, gently touching his lips.

"Ellington, trust me, I'm not whole, at least not yet. When I get better, I'll come back."

"Caitlin!"

"I have to go. Kiss Zoey for me, and tell the guys to behave." She turned away then stopped. Tears glistened in her eyes. "I love you," she whispered before she slipped out the door to the waiting taxi.

Epilogue

With all the drama that Yaz had gone through this past year, everything seemed to finally fall into place. Jim, Calvin, and Aunt Margaret were arrested. Jim and Dex got 20 years with no parole for kidnapping and attempted murder. His mother's murder was still unsolved due to lack of evidence, but they knew Jim Bailey was behind it. Calvin and Aunt Margaret got probation for their part in embezzling and fraud and Trish was back in New Orleans where she belonged.   Thanksgiving and Christmas were the best he ever had even if it was shared with the overprotective Howard brothers. He was awarded MVP for the Eastern Division Playoffs, and the Philadelphia Stallions were going to the Super Bowl, and his woman was cuddled up close to him where she belonged. It was time for them to start their forever. Their lovemaking was fierce and Zoey was a fast learner and admitted she loved being submissive, but only in the bedroom.

"Sassy," he whispered. She lifted her head to look at him. "You are my life, my next breath, a player's heart. Marry me so we can make a few more players."

"Too late, we already made one," she whispered and lifted his hand and placed it on her slightly rounded belly. Yaz grinned at her.

"Three months, that's all you have to plan our wedding and I wanted to it be grand."